Othe

MW00413411

The Train

"Tony explores one Southern boy's journey to the brink of manhood, bringing early memories to life with vivid descriptions, vibrant diction, and rhythmic syntax—a compelling read that shows you can't go wrong with a classics education."

Ruth Overman Fischer, PhD, George Mason University, Ret.

"Knows the human heart and the way of the world like Faulkner, writes like Hemingway!"

Col. Daniel W. Jacobowitz, USAF, Ret.

FLYING BLIND

FLYING BLIND

Tony Jordan

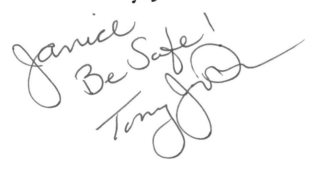

SPY HILL
PUBLISHING

Spy Hill Publishing

First Edition

Library of Congress Control Number: 2016901222
Spy Hill Publishing, Clinton, TN

ISBN-13: 9780692622247
ISBN-10: 0692622241

Book and cover design by Nathan Armistead
Printed in the United States of America

To Jake and the others I met on the road to Damascus,
and
to all those who ever supported a Combat Search and Rescue,
and
to all those nameless spies and spymasters who served our country,
many of whom are now stars on the wall at Langley

CONTENTS

PREFACE

THIS NOVEL BEGAN AS A series of short stories written over a period of two years. It is a collection of stories about flying, courage, altruism, and human interaction in a unique combat squadron—a squadron with a mission to save lives rather than take them.

"The Captain" is Jean-Louis Thibodeaux. Thibodeaux was introduced in my first novel—*The Train*—and appears in this book as the military pilot he subsequently became. After his stint with the Air Force in Indochina, Jean-Louis (like me) went on to become an officer with the Central Intelligence Agency, specializing in counterespionage. He is the primary character in *They've Crossed the Rubicon*, my upcoming novel about how an international conspiracy could subtly undermine the United States.

If Thibodeaux (pronounced "Tib-oh-doh") interests you, you can learn more of him and of his adventures in *The Train* and *They've Crossed the Rubicon*.

Acknowledgments

To Ruth and Jake for their support and encouragement throughout the creation of the short stories that eventually grew to become this book, and to Michele and Nathan Armistead for their invaluable assistance throughout the publication process.

FLYING BLIND

BETWEEN HEAVEN AND HELL

HE WOULD FREEZE IF HE could not find refuge. Hadn't they taught him how to make a snow cave in survival training? But if he stopped, he would freeze. If only he could see where he was going. He must be in an ice fog. He couldn't see ahead, but it was extremely bright, as if the sun was shining through the fog. He thought he could make it out. The sun was almost directly overhead, but that couldn't be. For it to be this cold, he would have to be too far north for the sun to be in that position. How did he get here? He was in Texas, wasn't he? Maybe he was in the panhandle. "It gets cold in the panhandle," he thought. He involuntarily shivered again. "Too cold."

He was very tired. He needed to sleep. Just a minute or two. If he could just stop. But somehow he knew he mustn't. He must go on, but it was so cold. He must stay upright. He kept going. Was that a sound?

It sounded like a muffled pounding. He could feel the vibrations. In the distance there was the sound of mumbled murmurings. Perhaps voices, but perhaps an ocean. There were no oceans in Texas. Maybe he was near the Gulf—but he could not be so cold at the Gulf. He searched his memory for somewhere so cold and barren but could only think of Dante, and the thought frightened him. Was his life so irredeemable that God would condemn him to the innermost circle of hell?

He couldn't remember how he had gotten from his airplane to this place. He must have ejected, but he didn't remember it. In fact, he couldn't actually remember being in the plane. His feeling was more akin to assuming he had been. If only the fog would lift, and he could see. The light was so bright it hurt his eyes. If it was the sun, he instinctively knew he must watch closely. They always came at you out of the sun. He, himself, always attacked out of the sun. But he couldn't seem to keep his eyes open. Yet he knew he must keep going. He did not feel out of breath, his muscles did not hurt, there was no pain—but he was so very sleepy, so very tired, and so very, very cold.

His head pounded. His mouth tasted of the vomit that stained the front of his uniform—the stink of which filled his nose so that he retched. His vision was blurred, but it began to clear as he rubbed his eyes. He held his wrist in front of his face. The hands of his watch indicated 0833. "Oh, shit!" he thought. It's after eight. They'll list me as AWOL. Dammit! Just one more way to screw me."

He looked around. He was in a hangar, but which one? He looked at the airplanes. None of them were T-38s. They were all different, but mostly they were T-39s. He must be in the transient hangar where they parked some of the aircraft visiting the base. The rest would be on the ramp outside. He was lying between two mechanic's chests that contained wrenches and ratchets. He was lying on something so uncomfortable that it seemed to be penetrating the small of his back. Rolling over, he shoved the pair of wire cutters toward the chest on his right.

He couldn't remember how he had gotten to the hangar. He remembered buying two six-packs of beer at the base exchange. He remembered that he needed to call Brenda. "Shit! Brenda!" he said aloud. But coming out through his dried and cracked lips it sounded more like, "Siiit! Endaaa!" He tasted his vomit and gagged, the back of his throat wanting to come to his lips. Had he talked to her?

Then he remembered. He had called her. She hadn't believed him, but he had the orders. He reached into his fatigue shirt pocket. The folded paper was wet from the vomit but he unfolded it and read again, "Airman Second Class Thomas Pickerton is ordered to report to Tan San Nhut Air Base, Republic of Vietnam for duty as a jet engine mechanic..." All the rest didn't matter. The bit about getting to Travis AFB California, the bit about authorized combat pay—none of that was important until you came to the part, "This order supersedes Special Order 665478 ordering A/2C Pickerton to Wiesbaden, Germany."

"Assholes! Change my orders. Tell me I can't marry my fiancée because I'm not a sergeant and I'm going to a combat zone. I mean, fuck! We had it all planned. I'll protest. They can't do this to me."

He was pissed. He had to find the first sergeant. But before that, he'd better get a fresh uniform and shower the vomit out of his hair. He staggered off towards the barracks area. He'd tell them he'd been sick in the night. That he had food poisoning. He'd go to the medical clinic. No, not the medical clinic, they might smell the beer. He'd claim he was so distraught by the new orders that he'd gotten sick. He'd show them the orders. They would believe him. What had Brenda said? That if he didn't want to marry her he should just say so. Don't blame the Air Force.

"Well, Goddamn it! It's the Air Force's fault!" he muttered, although it was unintelligible.

He was still in the fog, but it was not so cold. Perhaps hypothermia was setting in. Wasn't that what they had told him in survival training? Before you freeze, you begin to feel warm, and freezing is like going to sleep. He felt warmth returning, but now he seemed bound, unable to move. The light was still there, brighter than ever, but he still couldn't see through the fog. He kept going on, but now it was more difficult. There seemed to be resistance as he tried to lean forward into the fog. He was still so very tired. He sensed time had passed, but he didn't know how much. He didn't seem to be able to see his watch, but he knew it must be there. He wore it even when he slept, but he couldn't see it now. He tried, but couldn't get his arm in front of his face.

"Wait..." his mind paused. "Is that a voice? Relax. Take a deep breath and listen." He tried to expand his chest...he couldn't! Couldn't get his breath! He tried again, but again he could not. His chest moved less than an inch and then stopped. Now, he began to feel the pain. It seeped in. It was an itch, then a twitch, then an ache, then a burning sensation, and finally a conflagration of all his muscle, sinew, and bone. He didn't know bones could hurt, but his did. And now, even his soul burned as the pain tried to contort his body. But he could not move. Something pressed on his chest. His arms were restricted. His legs felt encased. He could breathe only in short gasps. He was no longer cold. His bones were burning.

"I can't breathe!" he gasped between intakes. "I can't breathe!" The pain was ever increasing. Then, briefly, he saw eyes. They were brown. Just eyes.

Somewhere a voice said, "What are you doing awake? Calm down, Lieutenant. I'm going to give you..." If it was supposed to be soothing, it wasn't. It was more a command, not unlike something he had heard in officer training.

But he couldn't concentrate. He needed focus, but his eyes would not. Nor would his mind. Neither body nor mind would respond to his will. He wanted the pain to go away, but it would not. He wanted to move, but he could not. Fleetingly, between his gasps for breath, he rejected the thought of Dante. This was Milton's Lake of Fire. Then the fog got heavier. What he thought were voices again faded into the murmur of a distant ocean.

The barracks were empty and his roommate was gone. That was good, because the room was so small you could barely turn around when both people were there.

The thought struck him that he would be stuck in another barracks in Vietnam. He didn't know if he could take it. He had always been claustrophobic, and the little rooms they expected him to live in made him gasp for air. And, as a jet engine mechanic, he had to work every day in freezing cold, windowless rooms. He suddenly felt closed in, almost to the point of panic. That was why he wanted to go to Germany. He could marry Brenda and they could have an apartment off the base. He would still have to work in a closed room, but after hours he wouldn't have to be confined, smelling the sweat of others and listening to stupid conversations about women, cars, and sex.

He quickly showered, brushed his teeth, and put on fresh fatigues. He shoved his vomit-stained fatigues under the bottom bunk. He would wash them later.

His hair still wet, he ran back to the flight line where unusual vehicles were running up and down. Personnel scurried about. It was not the usual choreography of flight launch or recovery.

"Strange," he thought, "there aren't any aircraft in the air." He knew the morning training launches were scheduled for 0630 and there should be aircraft in the pattern and lots of activity as the first launch recovered and the second launch taxied for take off. Instead there were fire engines and pickup trucks everywhere. Someone had had an emergency. No one seemed to have missed him.

He saw Harrison and asked him where the first sergeant was.

"Where've you been?" The question was more casual than accusative.

"Ahhh...." His still-clouded mind searched for an excuse. "In the hangar straightening out some tool chests somebody left all messed up. What's going on out here?"

"Geez, man. You must have heard it. I actually saw it. That F-5 that came in yesterday from Cannon...he was leaving this morning. He had a nose gear problem and tried to come back in. They foamed the runway at five thousand feet but he never even made it to the foam. Drug his right wing on touchdown and...geez, man! I've never seen anything like it. He pivoted on his wing, then his nose, then his tail, then his nose, tail, nose... *three times* he cartwheeled it down the runway. He came to a stop just short of the foam."

"Did the pilot die?"

"Don't know. They took him out of the cockpit and last I heard they were taking him to Wilford Hall over at Lackland. But that was hours ago. How didn't you hear all the commotion?"

"Oh, I always wear ear protectors, even in the hangar. Don't want to lose my hearing. Shit, man! That's something. Bad day for the pilot. Where's the first sergeant?"

"Uh, he's over at the line maintenance office, but I wouldn't bother him now. Seems like another of the transient aircraft had a problem and they were going to let it use the T-37 runway on the other side of the base. Then a T-39 taxiing over reported a problem with his gyro. Maintenance thought it might be a loose wire, but when they traced the circuit it turned out the wire had been cut along with a bunch of others. So the first sergeant's supervising a look at all the other aircraft parked in the transient area. He's kind of pissed. I wouldn't mess with him right now."

"But, man…I have to see him. He has to do something about these orders."

"Oh yeah. Well, congrats. I heard you got Germany. That's great."

"No, man. The fucking Air Force changed the orders to Tan San Nhut yesterday. I got to see the first sergeant about getting them changed back."

"Bummer, man! Too bad. Well, like I said, he's over in the line maintenance office. Good luck."

As Pickerton entered the maintenance office, the first sergeant was yelling orders over the FM radio set. He almost screamed as he told this unit and that to get over to such-and-such airplane.

"We think we've narrowed it to the nose well areas. Check the wiring in the nose wells. Look at every single airplane on the line. T-38s, transients, everything!"

The first sergeant turned to the base commander. "T-37 flight line is shutting down, sir. All aircraft aloft are being recalled and given straight-in landing instructions. All aircraft on the ground are being checked."

"How many so far?" the base commander asked.

"Eight, sir. I suspect that when they examine the wreckage of Aggressor 09 they'll find wires cut in the nose wheel well. Probably the wires to the shimmy damper on the nose gear and the worm gear activator for locking the wing gear in place. That would account for both the stuck nose gear and the failure of the right main on touchdown. Do we know anything about the pilot?"

"He's in surgery and will be for some time. I don't know the details, but he's in pretty bad shape."

The base commander asked for the list of aircraft on which inspections had found the damaged wires and, using his walkie-talkie, asked his executive officer to contact the wing commander's office and set up a briefing so he could bring him up to date. As he did, three individuals in plainclothes entered the office. Each wore in his suit coat chest pocket the badge of the Air Force Office of Special Investigations—OSI. "I wonder on whose authority these guys are here?" the base commander asked himself.

The OSI officers immediately began questioning the first sergeant, who held up his hand commanding them to stop, and then, with the same hand, pointed to the base commander. The special agents turned and surrounded the senior officer.

The burning had stopped, and while he sensed that his feet were once again freezing cold the rest of his body seemed as if it did not exist. He continued to hear the murmurings, and once or twice he felt as if the earth moved under him. It was almost as if a large animal was walking nearby. There was a thump and he shook, a wait, another thump, and he shook again. But always there was the fog. The fog through which he could not see, the fog that distorted sound, the fog that had borne with it freezing cold and insufferable heat and pain.

No longer did he have a sense of time or place. Even being was questionable. If he could not see or hear, did he exist? "I think, therefore I am," passed through his mind as if a branch carried in a flooded stream. He could not concentrate, but he was aware. Was that thinking? Did that qualify as existence? Attempts to capture and dwell on complete thoughts failed. It was as if he was sitting in a theater watching a feature length presentation of a film made up of one or two frames from thousands of completely disassociated movies.

"God," he wondered. "Where is God?" Images of Bible stories flashed through his mind. Moses on Sinai, Jesus on the cross, the Red Sea parting, Jesus looking down on the world with the devil. Too fast. They went too fast, but they differed from the other images. These were in technicolor. Then back into monochrome—where images continued to streak through his mind. Mr. Chips, Dreyfus, Robert Jordan, Jake Barnes, Frankie in his iron lung, an unknown cripple on crutches. All sped away, but left their traces—not on his mind, but on his soul. He felt as if his heart would ache if he could but feel it. Still, his soul felt, and it ached.

Pickerton, thinking it best not to bother the first sergeant at that particular moment, reported to his line chief who put him to work going through parked aircraft looking for wires that had been cut. He pulled the nose gear door downward and wedged his head and upper torso into the wheel well. Awkwardly, he brought his flashlight up while his free hand searched for anything that looked out of place. He found nothing on the first aircraft or the second. His third aircraft was a T-39 parked at the end of the transient parking area. It had been ignored by earlier inspectors because it had an engine cowling open and there were engine stands next to it.

Looking up into the well, he noticed a yellow wire that bowed out from its bundle. Reaching up, he pulled gently on it, and it came away from the bundle. The end of the wire had definitely been cut. He tugged gently on other wires in the bundle and three more came out.

Extracting himself from the wheel well he called out, "Over here! I've got some cut wires."

His line chief and four or five other mechanics arrived on the run. The line chief edged his way into the nose well to look, and, pulling out, said, "Yep, same as the others. Not just cut, but stuck back into the bundle so that a cursory inspection wouldn't detect any damage. Son of a bitch knew what he was doing. He didn't intend for any of these things to be found on the ground. We were lucky, I guess, about that T-39 gyro."

"Well, not everybody was lucky," interjected one of the sergeants. "How about the pilot of Aggressor 09?"

"Well, except him," the line chief answered. "But it could have been a whole lot worse if these other aircraft had gotten airborne."

The pain had returned. Not like before, but enough. It taunted him, almost as if it was daring him to move or think about it. The bright overhead sun had gone away and the murmurs had become voices once more. He tried to turn his head to see who spoke, but could not. He tried to lift his arm in front of his face to look at his watch, but could not. He still found himself breathing in short gasps and trying not to panic because he could not draw a deep breath.

He was still very tired and drifted in and out of consciousness. Each time he woke, his eyes focused just a little better. He tried to talk, but felt as if his mouth was full of sand. He was terribly thirsty. Never had he been thirstier. It was a new and uncomfortable experience. But then, so was the pain.

No longer did images rush through his mind. He could think coherently enough, but still had no answers and very few clues. The ceiling was asbestos tile with thousands of little holes. It was semi-dark, or was it semi-light? The voices were voices, but they remained unintelligible. There was a door—he could tell because the light changed as it opened and closed. He could see the shadow the door cast on the ceiling.

He tried to speak, but his lips seemed not to move to his command. A grunt emerged from his throat. More eyes peered down at him. They were clearer now. There was a mask—a surgical mask—below the eyes. It spoke:

"Lieutenant Thibodeaux, welcome back. We thought you might have wandered away from us, but you're going to be fine."

The voice faded and the eyes seemed to recede into a long tunnel through which he was moving backwards with an ever-increasing speed. As the tunnel grew longer and longer, he felt time passing. The tunnel was time, it must be. He was moving through time, stopping occasionally at stations along the way only long enough for a pair of eyes above a mask to speak to him briefly. Still, each time they confirmed to him that he continued to exist.

The pain seemed to recede as he whizzed through the tunnel but grow stronger the nearer he came to each stop. Anticipating the stops, he tried hard to ignore the pain. He wanted—no, needed—to speak with the mask and the eyes. He needed information, but the pain kept him from speaking. And then he left the station again, moving backwards, increasing his speed through time.

"They're definitely your fingerprints, Airman Pickerton. We found vomit on the floor and vomit on the fatigue uniform under your bunk. We found your wire cutters near the vomit in the hangar. They have only your fingerprints on them. There are beer bottles behind the tool chests. They have your fingerprints as well. Would you like to tell us what happened?"

"I don't know what happened. I remember talking to Brenda. She yelled at me and accused me of having the Air Force change my orders so I wouldn't have to marry her. I remember going to the hangar to have a beer because alcohol isn't allowed in the barracks and I can't stand being confined in that shoebox they call a semi-private room. It isn't big enough for one person and it doesn't have a window. It's just a closet really, but so are all the other so-called 'rooms' in the barracks." He almost spit when he said "rooms."

"Then I woke up, looked at my watch, and realized I was late for duty. I went back to the barracks, took a shower, put on some clean fatigues and reported to the flight line. I had to see the first sergeant about getting my orders changed. That's it. Maybe somebody came in and gave me the wire cutters or put them under me while I was asleep. Honest! I don't remember anything else." He tried to rise from the chair but the OSI agent grabbed him by the shoulder and forced him back down.

Another agent knocked on the door, entered, and handed the special agent in charge a piece of paper.

"Well, I'm sorry, Airman, but your fingerprints were found all over the wheel wells and gear doors of all the aircraft where we found cut wires. The Air Force will provide you a lawyer."

Turning to the agent who had just entered he said, "Tell the JAG we'll be ready for an Article 32 hearing this afternoon."

"How long?"

"What?"

"How long?"

"If you mean how long have you been here, the answer is three weeks."

"Three weeks? How could it be just three weeks? It seems like decades—or maybe eons. I thought I passed through centuries in the tunnel." He mumbled almost incoherently, but not so badly the doctor didn't know what he was saying.

"Yes, morphine can do that to you. But it's only three weeks."

"Only three weeks," Thibodeaux said weakly. "Only three weeks."

The doctor was standing above him. There was no mask now. The face seemed older, but to Thibodeaux at the age of twenty-two, most faces seemed older. The hair was salt and pepper. The eyes were not brown, but blue-green. These were not the eyes he had seen before, nor was the voice the one that had greeted him at many of the stations along the tunnel.

The doctor was shining light from a small pen into his eyes. He wanted him to follow the light with his eyes. Having learned just last night that his eyes were the only part of his body—other than his lips—that could move, he tracked the light as if it was his intended target in an air combat engagement.

Fighting against the constant pressure under his chin, he spoke through gritted teeth. "How long before I can return to flying?"

"Flying?" The doctor's voice carried a certain incredulity. "I think you had better think about sitting up before you consider flying."

Not one for dwelling on what he couldn't do, Thibodeaux started to explain to the doctor what a waste it would be if the top graduate in his pilot training class—the one with the highest scores *ever* in undergraduate pilot training—did not return to the cockpit. At that moment, however, technicians arrived with a device to go behind the bed, and the doctor was required to move.

It was a mirror that slanted forward. Now Thibodeaux could see to the foot of the bed and beyond. Although he had no significant peripheral vision because the cast encased the sides of his head, his field of vision was no longer restricted to just the ceiling tiles. He looked again, constructing a larger image by extrapolating from what he saw and what he perceived with his hearing. There was no bed across from him, but he sensed a bed to his right. The edge of a doorjamb was visible at the extreme left of the mirror so he knew there was a door to his left. Yes, he knew everything was reversed in the mirror—but not in its relation to his bed or his head.

He had no wife or family in Texas, so there was no one to come and describe for him other things. He would have to coax nurses and orderlies into taking time to describe his surroundings. He knew his father and mother were there somewhere, but he wouldn't want them to remain at his side. He was alive, and things would be what they would be. He had to master these challenges himself, and he certainly didn't want to talk to his father about returning to Mobile and entering the family "business." Not now.

He could see himself at the lower part of the mirror by cutting his eyes upward. His face retained traces of bruising with purplish black patches of blood not yet absorbed. His head was held in a plaster collar that extended up beyond his ears, and the constant pressure under his chin was part of a harness that disappeared somewhere north of his head. He was obviously in traction. The plaster cast extended downward, shrouding his entire body, including both shoulders.

He could feel air moving across his left forearm, and he could move that appendage slightly, flexing the fingers in his hand. But he could not move the upper arm at all. His right arm was immobilized, covered to his fingertips in plaster. He could feel the plaster on his right leg, and now could see it went all the way to his toes. His couldn't move his left leg but it didn't seem to have any plaster on it. Thinking about it, he realized there would probably be weights on both legs if he was actually in traction, and it appeared he was.

Well, at least he could see to the door using the new mirror. He tried to be casual—even jocular—but the image he could now see frightened him. It was as if a cold black shadow passed through his soul. In his mind all he could see was Frankie in his iron lung, trying to joke as he looked backwards through his mirror. He hadn't spoken to Frankie since visiting him in that hospital; the family had moved away and when they went back to visit no one in the hospital could—or perhaps it was, would—tell him anything about Frankie. Would that happen to him?

"It's a real waste you know," the first sergeant said to his collected minions. "He was a really good jet mechanic. You know, she not only didn't come to his court martial, she refused to read his letters. She sent them all back unopened."

"Yeah," the team lead said. "She's a real bitch. You know he had a year of college before he joined? He enlisted because he wanted to marry her and it was the fastest way to get an income. So he gives up college to marry her and then she stiffs him when this happens. He may have been a pretty smart guy otherwise, but his decisions about women were pretty bad."

"'Pretty smart' guys don't get drunk and cut wiring bundles on Air Force aircraft and then not remember what they did," the first sergeant observed.

"So what happens to him now?" asked one of the mechanics.

"Leavenworth," the first sergeant answered. "That's where they send all the long term military prisoners."

"Twenty years is a long time."

"Yeah, but he's only twenty-one now, so he'll just be forty-one when he comes out. Age-wise it's like serving twenty in the Air Force and then retiring," the team lead mused.

"True," said the first sergeant. "But when he 'retires' he'll have a criminal record and a dishonorable discharge to overcome. It'll be tough. You know though, he might be out in fifteen years if they give him parole. Maybe even ten."

Everyone agreed it was a tragedy and went back to work. The break was over.

Having no knowledge of what other people thought about him, Pickerton regarded himself as a betrayed lover, and more, as a betrayed loyalist. Even his parents had disowned his behavior. Good boy gone bad. They blamed the girl. They had never liked her all through high school. They were sure she would tell him she was pregnant to get him to marry her. And even though that hadn't happened, when he dropped out of college to join the Air Force they knew it was only a matter of time before other bad things happened. Their anger only fed his anger. Although in the back of his mind he knew he alone was responsible, he could not yet admit it to himself. He used self-pity to defend against the stares and innuendoes of others while they processed him through the various levels of military discipline until he was escorted into a cell at Fort Leavenworth Federal Prison. The windowless box was six feet wide by ten feet long. It held a narrow bunk and a toilet. That was it. There was one shelf above the bunk. Rather than bars along the front—as he had seen in movies about prisons—there was a solid steel door that had a reverse peep hole and a sliding partition through which he could receive trays or books or, if necessary, place his hands for handcuffs.

He would remain in this cell until authorities moved him to a different section of the prison so he could interact with some of the other prisoners. They thought he might be at risk because the normal thieves and murderers in Leavenworth took a dim view of spies and saboteurs. He was there because he had been charged with, and had pled guilty to, sabotage of government equipment. It would take time before he might be accepted into the general population. If ever.

The first night he felt as if he could not move. It was as if the ceiling was pressing on his chest. It was darker than he feared. No light found its way into the cell. He found breathing difficult. The walls restricted him on all sides. His breath came in gasps. He wanted to claw his way out but he could not. They had buried him alive. If he did not die, surely he would go crazy. He would appeal! This was torture, and they weren't allowed to torture him. It was that thought that helped him through the night, and the light was turned on the next day. At least he thought it was the next day. Already he had lost track of time.

"Good morning, Lieutenant, sir!" A cheerful voice if ever he had heard one. Standing at the foot of the bed was an individual in blue regulation hospital pajama pants and a blue and white seersucker robe. He was leaning on two crutches. He was young, with dark hair cut in regulation style, although a wayward lock kept falling over his left eyebrow. Above his broad smile there were two dark, extremely bright, eyes. Hanging from his shoulder and across his body was what appeared to be a newsboy's canvas bag.

"Airman First Class Fowler at your service. You need, I fetch. Something to read today?"

Through his clenched teeth, Thibodeaux responded, "Not quite sure how I would hold a book. Little encumbered at the moment."

"Uh, what was that, sir? It's a little difficult to understand you. Just a minute."

He maneuvered his crutches and almost immediately stood leaning over Thibodeaux's face. This close he looked even younger. Thibodeaux wondered if he was even shaving yet.

"Ok sir, let's try that again."

"I said, I don't think I can handle a book," Thibodeaux grunted, the traction strap under his chin keeping his teeth closed.

"Oh, that's no problem, sir. I also read. So, if there's something you want to hear, I can give you half an hour in the morning, and maybe a little less in the evening. I'll have to check my schedule book." With that, he drew a small black book from his bag. "Yes, sir. Half an hour in the mornings, and I can pencil you in for some time each evening when they take Captain Komenda to hydrotherapy."

"What day is it?" Thibodeaux grunted.

"Tuesday, sir. We'll have turkey soup and rice on the lunch trays."

"No, what's the date?"

"Does it really matter, sir? The date is only relative to those on the outside. For those of us in here, it's Tuesday, and we'll get turkey soup and some banana pudding."

Strangely, Thibodeaux understood.

"Say, sir, I hear you stayed on the bull, but it landed on you."

"What?"

"Just a figure of speech, sir. I'm from Wyoming, where we try to ride bulls in rodeos. Sometimes a cowboy stays on the bull, but the bull falls on him and the cowboy gets injured. Way they tell the story, you stayed on the bull, but it fell on you."

Thibodeaux thought about it a moment. "Yes, I guess that's so. Sometimes you do everything right and the bull falls on you."

Fowler smiled. "That's good, Lieutenant. Glad to see you don't feel sorry for yourself. Too many guys in here do, you know. Like that major down the hall. There's no getting that guy out of the wallow he's made for himself. Couple of broken legs is all, and you'd think he was dying. I guess his problem is that everybody else up here is aircraft-related and his was a car wreck. And, confidentially, I hear he was drunk when he did it. So now he's here with all these hero types, and he doesn't know what to do, so he sulks and complains about being put in with junior officers and enlisted men."

Thibodeaux listened, but quickly grunted out, "Fowler, I'm not sure I'd go around carrying stories, especially about field grade officers. Might get you in trouble. I mean, what if I told somebody what you said?"

"Right, sure, sir. I understand, but, I mean, what are they going to do? Put me in a helicopter and send me to Vietnam? Been there, done that, got the T shirt." At this he pulled his robe open, displaying a green T-shirt with a green hornet silk-screened on it. Around the hornet was printed in gold, "20th Special Operations Squadron—Green Hornets."

Closing the robe, he continued, "Besides, sir, how else are you going to get things to think about if I don't keep you up on all the scuttlebutt? After all, I'm the only ambulatory person on this ward. So listen, there's a nice little library on the second floor. What can I get you to read—as in, what can I get to read *to* you?"

"How about today's paper?" Thibodeaux growled through his teeth.

"No, sir, no paper reading. I don't like reading news and you won't like hearing it. Just makes you irritated. No, sir. Philosophy, theology, engineering, murder, mayhem, but no news. Not good for your healing process."

"So, now you're a doctor?"

"Oh, no, sir. Wouldn't ever want to be a doctor. It's way too sad a profession for me. I just want to go back to Wyoming and raise horses. But, if I've learned nothing else in my short Air Force career, it's that worrying about things over which you have no control doesn't do you, or those around you, any good. It's like, why would you go and poke a stick at a nest of rattlesnakes? You're better off ignoring them and getting the hell out of the area."

"Ok, so no newspapers," Thibodeaux grunted. "What do you suggest?"

"Well sir, Captain Komenda is reading this book on philosophy by Michel de Montaigne. I'm learning a lot from it. Mostly it's just common sense, but, like, you never think about it. Sure helps a lot for people who don't get out much. Then, there's this fellow Camus. We read him last month. He's got an interesting take on life. Doesn't believe in God, he says, but somehow I'm not really convinced. He has a lot to say because he was in a sanatorium for TB for a good amount of time. He didn't get around much, kind of like you. Of course there's always Agatha Christie or one of the other crime and mystery writers. Pick your poison." He laughed at his joke. Thibodeaux got it, but only groaned.

"So who's Captain Komenda?" Thibodeaux asked.

"He's my pilot. We were crew on Green Hornet 35. He was the aircraft commander, Lieutenant Mead was the copilot, and I was the crew chief and door gunner. That's how we ended up in here. We got shot down up by Thuy Wah while attacking what we thought was a small fuel dump. Turned out to be a truck park with multiple ZSU-23s defending it. Lieutenant Mead didn't make it. I got this." He gestured with his head towards his right leg.

"Captain Komenda took the stick in his head and crushed the front part of his skull. He also broke his back. They put a plate in his head and fused his spine and now they're teaching him to walk again. He swears he'll fly again, but I don't know." Fowler shifted himself on his crutches, easing the plastered leg to a more comfortable position. "Every time they take him outside he has terrible headaches from the cold affecting the plate in his head. He says it just takes some getting used to, and willpower. Captain Komenda is a great believer in willpower. Anyway, he's my pilot so I have to take care of him. Might as well do what I can for everybody else who's up here while I'm at it. It's not like you guys can run down to the library on your own. These crutches make me mobile, and I can maneuver on them about as well as I can walk in a pair of boots with riding heels." To demonstrate he pirouetted on one crutch catching himself with the second and swinging back into a position next to the bed. This, of course, went completely unnoticed by Thibodeaux who lost sight of Fowler the moment he quit bending over the head of the bed.

"So, then, do we call you Mercury or Hermes?"

"Mercury or Hermes?" Fowler's voice rose in a question at the end.

"Sure. Hermes was the Greek messenger of the Gods, and Mercury was what the Romans called him. Obviously the reading you and Captain Komenda have been doing hasn't included mythology."

"Say, isn't there a tie made by somebody called Hermes?" Fowler asked, somewhat unsure of himself.

"Absolutely. Hermes is a big Parisian *haute couture* place. Ties, scarves, purses, jackets—everything a well-dressed lady or gentleman could need as an *accoutrement*." Thibodeaux's French sounded less like a practiced second language, and more like the noise a rutting pig makes. Although his grunting

English was understandable, his clenched-teeth French sounded like German or Slavic. But Fowler got the idea.

"Well, I guess we better go with Mercury. I think I'd rather be known by the name of a high-class Ford than some polka-dot tie."

"Ok, well then, Mercury, I'll listen to whatever you want to read. Now fly off to where ever it is you have to be."

Thibodeaux was tired. This was the most he had talked since waking from the surgeries. The pain was getting worse, but he knew they would come with the morphine in a little while. His awareness of the morphine bothered him. Perhaps he should have more willpower and less morphine. Maybe Captain Komenda was right. Well, he would give it some thought—maybe lots of thought. He had the time.

Fowler swung off, and Thibodeaux saw in his mirror the bottoms of the crutches and his heels as he cleared the door. "Heels," thought Thibodeaux. "How appropriate. But he uses crutches instead of wings."

And so they read and talked. Fowler was there promptly each morning, his book in the bag. He would place himself in a leaning position over Thibodeaux's left shoulder, wedged between the bed frame and the wall so that he had both hands free to hold the book. He would read, stopping often to discuss this passage or that thought. In addition, he offered stories about Wyoming, or what he would do when he collected all the back pay the Air Force owed him. He told Thibodeaux what the weather was outside and how lucky they were to be inside, and always he talked about how Captain Komenda was doing. Of course, Thibodeaux had never met Komenda, or, for that matter, any of the other denizens of the orthopedic floor, but he knew each one in detail through Mercury's uncanny narrative ability. He knew those who left and those who came. Only once did one of them, a captain in a wheelchair, stop by on his way out to whatever the world had become since Thibodeaux had been confined.

"Been hearing from Fowler for weeks there was a baby fighter pilot up here." His chair was at the foot of Thibodeaux's bed. He couldn't have been more than thirty, but he looked seventy. His face was thin and worn. His eyes betrayed a man who had experienced a great deal of pain. He was wearing a leather contraption that encircled his waist and from which emanated ascending metal spokes that curved back in at his neck. His head was held upright and rigid by the brace that encircled his head at the chin and under the ears.

"Now that they're sending me home on convalescent leave, thought I'd stop by for a personal reconnaissance. Johnson, F-105s. Thirty-Sixth Fighter Squadron out of Korat. Lost a race with a SAM over northern Laos and punched out. Broke my blasted back. Going too fast when I pulled the handles."

By now able to be heard through his teeth at a distance greater than a foot or so, Thibodeaux answered:

"Thibodeaux, F-5s. First Aggressors out of Cannon. Gear collapsed. Sabotage they tell me. Guess I broke my back as well. Neck, shoulder, leg…name it, it's broken. Hell, I think I broke my tailbone." He forced what he hoped sounded like a laugh.

"Well, I'd like to stay and swap lies, but you'd be at a disadvantage since you can't use your hands—and besides, my family is waiting on me downstairs." The captain paused then continued:

"Thibodeaux, I know we fighter pilots are all pretty tough guys and don't take advice very well, but let me give you some anyway. From what I hear, you're a pretty good guy. Smart and well-grounded. Remember that, when they come to change that cast. Remember it when they start your rehabilitation. Find your center. Concentrate. That roller coaster ride you took down the runway is going to seem like Disneyland compared to what's coming. If you think your instructors in pilot training were sadistic bastards, wait 'til you meet your physical therapists. But remember, just like the instructors, they'll make you better. Keep putting in the corrective control responses in the proper sequence and eventually she'll come out of the spin. If she doesn't…well…you're dead, and then you don't care anyway. *Ding Hao*, Lieutenant."

"Thanks, I think," was all Thibodeaux could muster in reply. But, as the captain's wheelchair was disappearing from the mirror's edge, Thibodeaux grunted out, "Fly safe!"

The next morning, cheerful as ever, Fowler was there with more stories about who was being done unto on the ward.

"Why don't you go home?" Thibodeaux blurted the question completely out of the blue. In fact, it was like an attack out of the sun. Fowler never saw it coming. Thibodeaux had him in his sights and raked him nose to tail. Thibodeaux felt miserable the moment he asked. It was kind of like attacking some flier who had just dropped his gear to surrender.

"I'm sorry. Did you want me to leave?"

"No, I don't want you to leave. I want to know why you stay around so many miserable people. I want to know how you can be so goddamn cheerful. I want to know why you don't go home to Wyoming and be with your family."

"Well, aren't we in a mood this morning?" Fowler replied. "Gee, Lieutenant, I didn't know I got on your nerves so badly."

"Fowler, you don't get on my nerves. You're the one ray of sunshine in this otherwise Stygian world, but I honestly feel guilty if—in even a small way—I'm keeping you in this place."

"Lieutenant, you're not keeping me here. Captain Komenda isn't keeping me here. The doctors aren't keeping me here. I stay here because this is where my family is. In Wyoming, I've got a father who drinks but means well. He works on somebody else's ranch. My mother remarried a sheep farmer and they barely get by. For either one of them, having me move in would be a burden. I tried it for a week. I couldn't work, and having to take care of me only meant they had to give up something else they needed to be doing, just to make it all come out even. I mean, can you see me riding a horse, or roping a stray? Yeeehi! Git along, little dogie!" He slapped his leg cast with his hand.

"You know what we do in Wyoming when a horse breaks his leg? We shoot him. We shoot him because he isn't going to be of any use. All he'll do is take up stable space and eat the oats and hay that a productive horse could be using. Hell, sir, I can't even stock the shelves in a 7-Eleven.

"No, sir. This hospital is where my family is. Captain Komenda is like an older brother. He needs me. Hell, even you need me. Besides, on this ward, he who can move, commands. I'm the only one who can get around, so I'm not just an equal here, I'm a superior. Works out for just about everybody, wouldn't you say? Now, do you want to hear what's happened to that major down the hall with the broken legs?"

"It really isn't fair," he thought. "I'm paying for something I have absolutely no memory of doing. Something so far from my nature that I, myself, am disgusted by it." His breathing rate increased.

The cell seemed to close in on him. In the months he had been incarcerated he had noticed that the more distressed or agitated he became, the smaller the cell became. It became more difficult to breathe. During these episodes he could feel the cell move. It didn't collapse, it just moved, almost stealthily. He could swear it pinned him to the bunk. He was unable to rise, unable even to turn over. It pressed in on him. His breath came in gasps. He couldn't take a full breath. He panicked. He wanted to call out but could not. He tried to calm himself by concentrating on taking slower breaths, by telling himself it was all in his mind; that he was in no danger. Slowly the walls seemed to recede. His breathing returned to normal.

He must gain control of himself. It would, he thought, take time, but he had twenty years; no, less than that now. He could do it. His discussions with the prison psychologist and chaplain were helping. He knew he had to learn not to allow his emotions to drive his perceptions. He needed to become detached and objective. He had talked to the psychologist about self-hypnosis. He wondered if the prison library had any books about it. Maybe his parents could send him the books. He would study and learn to control himself. Wasn't it, after all, lack of control that had gotten him here? Maybe the psychologist could help him find ways to do it.

At the urging of the psychologist he wrote his parents, again apologizing for his actions and the embarrassment he had caused himself and the family. This time he explained his thinking about control and asked them to see if they could arrange for him to get some books on self-hypnosis. What else, then, did he need to do? He had apologized to his parents. Apologized to the Air Force and his unit. Perhaps he should apologize to that pilot who had been hurt. He didn't know how to get in touch with him. Maybe his parents or the prison chaplain could find out. What would he say in the letter? I'm sorry? Sounded more than a little lame. He could explain about Brenda...but that was just an excuse. Still, it was the truth, and wasn't there something about the truth setting you free? He would talk to the chaplain about how to write the letter, but first, maybe if he just tried...

He took his pencil and wrote, "Dear Lieutenant Thibodeaux..."

Like a piece of furniture, Thibodeaux lay there. He wondered that people didn't set coffee cups or glasses on him. His head was hidden by the plaster that extended, like the metal neck of an armored suit, up his neck to the top of his head. His feet were covered with a thin blanket of Air Force blue. His right arm was thrown outwards, the cast extending to his fingertips. The left arm exited the plaster at his biceps, but it was pinned to the side of his body with tubes in the veins. The plaster of the body cast went down to his crotch. He might as well be a coffee table or a credenza. Sure, they checked on him every so often, but most of the time he just lay there, listening, and looking into his overhead mirror at the foreshortened or elongated forms of people as they moved into and away from the focal point. People pretty much forgot he was there.

Thus it had been that Thursday. He knew it was Thursday because he had smelled the chicken soup on the cart as they wheeled it by. Thursday of some week after he had been there—how long? Still, as Fowler had predicted, weeks had become unimportant. It could have been months. He had little idea of time other than it was Thursday, definitely Thursday, because they had chicken soup. Two doctors had stopped at the door to the ward, unaware of their eavesdropper.

"Yes, but when are you going to tell him? He deserves to know." The first doctor spoke quietly.

"I don't know. I mean, I hate this part of the business. It sucks big time. I suppose I'll tell him when it becomes more obvious."

"Before you move him up to the seventh floor, I hope?"

"Of course, before I move him there. Everybody in the hospital knows that's hospice. Geez! I'm not so unfeeling that I would spring it on him and move him up all at the same time. I just want him to enjoy the little time he has left."

"Why don't you discharge him and let him go home? Isn't that what we do with ambulatory patients?"

"Dammit! I did that. He went home and came back a week later. He didn't want to be home. He wanted to be here, so I let him stay. I had him admitted as a cancer patient without his knowledge. He thinks he's back on the orthopedic floor."

"Well, all I can say is, it's a damn shame. Damned fine kid, hero and all that. Did you hear they want to give him the Air Force Cross? Seems that when he and Komenda were shot down, Fowler pulled Komenda out of the burning aircraft even though he had that shattered right leg. He tried to get the copilot as well, but he was already dead. Then he took his M-16 and held a bunch of North Vietnamese regulars at bay until the other helicopters could get in to rescue them. If he was an officer, I think they'd be giving him a Medal of Honor."

"Yes, I know all about that. He specifically said he didn't want the ceremony until after he's out of his cast and off of his crutches. It has something to do with returning to duty with Captain Komenda. And I suspect that's why he's back here. He's developed some sort of attachment to the captain and feels only he can take care of him. I've never really seen anything quite like it."

"Well, we both know Komenda isn't going back on active duty, so that's a nonstarter."

"Yes, and I think even Fowler knows that, but he isn't going to tell Komenda. It's a strange bond, but I think it does Komenda a world of good, and, Lord knows, it's given Fowler a purpose. So, as far as I'm concerned, we aren't going to meddle until we have to."

"Well, I agree with you, the whole thing sucks. We put nineteen pieces of bone back together to give him his leg only to discover bone cancer. Dammit! Sometimes I hate what we do."

The doctors moved away, but Thibodeaux now bore a secret that weighed on his heart so heavily he literally shrank within his cast. It wasn't just the muscle atrophy he was experiencing, somehow he felt himself physically diminished and morally exhausted.

Pickerton concentrated on his breathing. Letting go of his fear, he allowed it to fall as if from a great height. A height so remote that he lost sight of the fear as it fell to whatever was below. He sought to empty himself of thought. He could feel his heart beat. He sensed the pulsing of blood through his arteries and veins. It moved in waves, and each wave took him deeper into the aura of energy that surrounded him. He could exist like this forever, but what was forever? Time had no meaning for him. Today, yesterday, tomorrow...all were the same. For yesterday had been now, today was now, and tomorrow would become now. *Now* was important, and *now* he felt there was no need to control, no need to fear. There was only a need to be, and, in being, to allow all around him to be unto itself.

Still, there were things he understood that the "now" demanded if he were to honor the concept. He roused himself to once again attempt the letter to the lieutenant. Each time he tried, guilt rushed out of the void and crushed him under its weight. His breathing again came in gasps, and the walls began to slide downward and in. Yet each start gave him hope that one day he could do it. He could not forgive himself until he sought forgiveness from the lieutenant. Both the chaplain and the psychologist agreed. He must cast out that final demon before he could achieve peace and before he could hope to begin a true rebuilding of his life. Once again he tried..."Dear Lieutenant Thibodeaux..."

Thibodeaux attempted joviality when Fowler came to read. He called him Quick Silver, although in his mind he thought more of Hephaestus, the lame god misbegotten of Hera and Zeus. Still, Thibodeaux attempted humor. Fowler, he of uncanny ability, saw through it immediately. At first Fowler thought it a recurrence of the guilt Thibodeaux had earlier expressed about

Fowler staying in the hospital, but quickly realized it was something deeper than that.

"Ok, Lieutenant. I don't know how you found out since I know you can't get out of that bed…but out with it. You know, don't you?"

"Know what?"

"You know about my cancer."

"What cancer?"

"Lieutenant, you're not a good liar. You're not even a passable liar. You *know*."

"Hell, Fowler. I don't want to know. I didn't want to know. But when you're a log on the beach, all kinds of things happen to you. I'm really sorry. I didn't know you knew. In fact, I understood they hadn't told you."

"Told me? Listen, Lieutenant. Nurses and doctors come to *me* when they want to know what's happening on this ward. Heck, I knew the day they readmitted me. They sent me for a blood test and the tech was all apologies. Wanted to know if it hurt much and that sort of thing. That they didn't tell me about the cancer, and that they didn't suggest a treatment… that tells me everything else I need to know."

"But how do you do it?"

"Do what?"

"Stay so damned happy?"

"What's the alternative, sir? Do you want me to check into the seventh floor and sit around moaning about dying?"

"But Robert, I still don't understand." Thibodeaux used Fowler's Christian name for the first time in their exchanges.

"Lieutenant," Fowler never used first names, always ranks. "You know when we first met and I told you me and Captain Komenda were reading Montaigne? I told you Montaigne had a philosophy that was pretty much just common sense. Well, one thing he says is, 'unable to govern events, I govern myself.' Now that's the key, see? Everyone is responsible for himself. Now that guy Camus says that even if there is no god and no heaven or hell, we need to find a purpose in life. A purpose that is worthy of our life, since there's not going to be anything else. It's all pretty simple, really. See, heaven is this place we make ourselves. So is hell. And we're like walking on a beam suspended between the two. It's up to us as individuals whether we jump off on the heaven side, or fall off on the hell side. Still, I sometimes think about whether there really is a God. What do you think, sir? Is there a God?"

Unable to brush the tears from his eyes, Thibodeaux blinked several times to clear his vision and sniffed to unstop his nose. All of this was difficult with the chinstrap pulling his mouth closed.

"A God? I just turned twenty-three. How the hell would I know? I haven't got enough experience to tell you if the Taj Mahal is really white, or if draining water spins the opposite way in Australia; but yes, Fowler, I think there is a God. At this moment, he's not on my list of close friends. In fact, I think he's pretty much a son of a bitch; but yes, he, or she, or it…is there. If I thought I'd be happier in the world by denying him, I would do it. I have absolutely no idea how he applies to any of this, because God is an infinite concept and I am a finite being.

When I try to understand the infinite with my finite mind it only confuses me and makes my head hurt, so I guess your philosophy is the best we can do. But I'm really sorry, Robert. Really sorry."

"It's ok, sir. I'm not sorry. I've got a really good life. You couldn't ask for more. Friends, being needed, being useful, people who will remember me...Isn't that what we all want? Isn't it all we really need? Don't feel sorry for me, sir. I'm one of the lucky ones. I found a philosophy that works and I'm smart enough to know it. I just hope this bad leg doesn't give way when I go to jump off the beam." He smiled.

"Oh, before I forget, there was a letter for you at the nurse's station. I have it in my bag. Would you like me to read it?"

"Sure, whatever. It's probably from my mother."

"No sir, I don't think it's from your mother," Fowler said as he ripped the end from the envelope.

"Dear Lieutenant Thibodeaux..."

And so it went, each man balancing himself on the narrow beam he must traverse, suspended somewhere between Heaven and Hell.

CHAPTER 1

HEROES IN WAITING

THE ENGINES DRONED, OCCASIONALLY CHANGING pitch ever so slightly as the aircraft climbed or descended. The nylon sling seat felt like a rock outcropping. His legs had gone numb somewhere over the Gulf of Siam, and even short walks around the aircraft during stops at Takhli and Ubon had not restored full feeling. He wondered why they hadn't included this particular torture in one of the "resisting interrogation" training programs at the survival school. Certainly being strapped into a shoulder-width, rock-hard seat for hours at a time was enough to cause a person either to go crazy or to become willing to do anything to avoid being strapped in again.

He looked around the cargo hold of the C-130. Those who had gotten off to begin their tours had been replaced by those who were leaving at the end of their tours. There was a decided difference in the faces. Those arriving had looked uncertain—some even fearful. Those leaving looked—for the most part—happy. A few looked a little somber, but they were mostly happy.

Many had *sawatdi* plastic garlands hanging from their necks. The garlands were a Thai custom for leaving and arriving. *"Sawatdi"* in Thai was like *"aloha"* in Hawaiian. It meant both hello and goodbye. And, as in Hawaii, the Thai custom had originally been to place a lei of flowers around the neck when bidding welcome or farewell. But technology had overtaken the tradition in Thailand, and now the leis were narrow plastic strips adorned with roundels of crimped plastic that, once someone explained it, did resemble flowers. The leis could be had for very few *baht* at innumerable stalls in any village close to an air base. He wasn't sure he liked the plastic, but still, he guessed it was the thought that counted.

When he had departed Clark Air Base in the Philippines that morning, his khaki uniform had been freshly starched and pressed. He could have cut himself on the creases in his trousers and shirt. Now the khakis were a sweat-stained, wrinkled ensemble that resembled pajamas more than a military uniform. He wore his nylon summer flying jacket over his short-sleeved shirt because, while in the air, the C-130 compartment was like an icebox. When the aircraft landed at each base along its route, he took the jacket off because the temperature and humidity were so high outside he could easily overheat on his walks around the tarmac. He felt sorry for those who had not known beforehand that the C-130's cargo deck would be so cold at altitude. Those shivering souls had huddled, arms crossed in their small seats, attempting to warm themselves. He had also brought his flight line hearing protectors, or, as they were euphemistically known, Mickey Mouse ears. Worn over the earplugs handed out to all the passengers, his "MM" ears further muted the mind-numbing roar of the four turboprop engines.

For about the thirtieth time that day, events of the past three years cycled through his mind like clips from a black and white movie. College graduation, pilot training, jet fighter training, assignment to the aggressor squadron, the accident—no, it wasn't an accident—someone had sabotaged his aircraft. The hospital, the body cast, the rehabilitation, the attempt and failure to return to fighters because his surgically repaired back could no longer tolerate the fighter's g-forces. But he could fly helicopters—and here the image of his first helicopter solo flashed on the screen at the back of his mind. Then rescue training and the secret meetings. Finally, jungle survival school, and at last, assignment to an active combat rescue squadron responsible for flying rescue missions in Cambodia, Laos and North Vietnam.

He had joined the Air Force to fly jet fighters and to become a test pilot. Somewhere, somehow, somebody had spilled ink on that blueprint. Nowhere in his plans had there been helicopters or secret missions for the government. Nowhere had there been a template for the torture of immobility in a body cast, or pain so severe he had begun to understand the concept of the everlasting fires of hell. A good thing he had studied Stoicism as a child and in college. Was there some *reason* all these unimagined occurrences had conspired against his original plans? Perhaps, perhaps not. At this point it was all guesswork. Only at the end of life did he expect the answer might be found—and he was nowhere near the end. At least he hoped he wasn't.

Once more the engines changed pitch as the aircraft began its descent toward Nakhon Phanom, Thailand, also known as NKP. This was his stop. The C-130 taxied to a parking spot in front of base operations and, as the engines began to shut down, the rear ramp lowered. After the load-master gave the thumbs up, he undid his seat belt. His legs were so numb he rose only with great difficulty. As he passed through the back of the aircraft he stopped to retrieve a duffel bag that had been piled with other luggage in the rear. Other pilots, like the F-105 pilots who had deplaned at Takhli, carried B-4 suitcases, but he favored the duffel bag because it carried much more than the B-4. So he looked like an enlisted guy, no big deal. Right there, stenciled on the side of the bag it said:

Capt. J. L. Thibodeaux
USAF

Taking up his helmet bag and throwing the duffel over his shoulder, he walked down the ramp into the pungent, wet heat. People milled about, searching for their bags. Other aircraft were running up their engines, taxiing to and fro, arriving and departing the airdrome. He saw everything through a miasma of burning jet fuel exhausting into the hot, moist air, moving in shimmering waves across blacktop radiating over a hundred degrees. Buildings—both close and distant—lost their solidity as their images bent and danced through the swirling, undulating heat. They seemed more mirage than reality. This was his element. He loved the sticky, sweet smell of the burning jet fuel. The heat and humidity reminded him of his home on the Gulf Coast.

He passed a group of four outgoing passengers walking toward the C-130. Like him, they were wearing khakis, three captains and a first lieutenant. All wore pilot's wings. Each was draped with plastic leis. One had more than twenty hanging around his neck. Each of the others had at least ten. "Very popular people," he thought.

Behind the six-foot chain link fence separating the flight line from the rest of the base, a large group of aircrew in flight suits, fatigues, and green baseball caps cheered as the departing pilots walked to the aircraft. Twice the pilots stopped, turned, and waved. The cheering sounded a little like it might have been fueled by a dram or so of alcohol.

At the gate, a sergeant stopped him and asked for his orders. He handed over a copy and then passed through, into the throng of green-hatted revelers. Once among the throng he realized there was no doubt. Alcohol was part of the—should he term it—celebration. It certainly seemed a festive gathering, especially since there were champagne bottles being waved about.

A junior colonel, sweat staining his cotton flight suit, looked at the stenciled name on the duffel and pronounced, "Ah, new blood! Welcome, Captain Thibodeaux. Welcome to Rescue! Welcome either to paradise or the upper reaches of hell—if you're a Milton kind of guy. It's all relative."

It was April. At least that's what it was in the United States. In Thailand, nobody cared whether it was April, May, or June—and the year was of no importance at all. Time was measured in days until you went home. Home, of course, was a euphemistic word, mainly meaning anywhere but Thailand. So Jean-Louis Thibodeaux had 365 days until he went home.

Unless, of course, he went home earlier in a medevac aircraft or, God forbid, a body bag.

"Have some champagne, Captain." A very tall, sandy-haired first lieutenant held out a bottle of cheap champagne toward Jean-Louis.

The young colonel intercepted it and said, "No alcohol for Captain Thibodeaux. He's flying later. In fact, Stretch, you should knock off now as well."

The very tall lieutenant responded to the use of his nickname—or in aviation terminology, call sign—by narrowing his eyes ever so slightly, turning his head a bit to the right, and looking down at the five-foot-ten squadron commander. "Yes, sir," he answered. Nothing more. No questions of why, or protestations that his name wasn't on the flying schedule for another two days. Just a simple, "Yes, sir."

Stretch took the champagne bottle from the colonel and handed it to another of the green-hatted crowd. Then, using his height to look over the crowd, he found and moved towards a sergeant at the edge of the fifty or so boisterous revelers. Leaning down—for at six foot seven he was much taller than the five-foot-seven flight engineer—he whispered something that precipitated a knowing nod from the sergeant. The sergeant moved through the crowd, singled out two PJs—pararescue jumpers—and gave them a sign to slip away from the gathering.

It wasn't far from base operations to the headquarters of the rescue squadron, and the three walked there in five minutes. Still, a five-minute walk in the heat and humidity was sufficient to leave them soaking wet, front and back. Salt stains began to appear on their fatigues. The air-conditioning inside the building made it feel like a walk-in freezer, intensifying their awareness of their wetness and their uncontrollable shivers.

They passed into the squadron briefing room and waited, unconsciously rubbing their hands together against the wet, cold air blowing from the two wall-mounted air conditioners. The chrome metal arms and plastic seat covers of the chairs and couches emphasized the freezer-like quality of the room. Waiting with them was the squadron's administrative noncommissioned officer in charge, Master Sergeant Williamson. He carried a folder of forms.

Lieutenant Colonel Nathaniel B. Schaffer invited Captain Thibodeaux to join him in the squadron commander's pickup truck. Thibodeaux's duffel bag was thrown into the bed and Thibodeaux slipped into the passenger seat, banging his knee on the UHF and VHF radio consoles installed under the dash. Windows up and air conditioner on, Colonel Schaffer looked serious.

"Thibodeaux, what the hell is going on? I get visited by an O-6 from Rescue Headquarters who instructs me to identify my most trustworthy and capable night recovery trained copilot, flight engineer and pararescue team. Then he tells me to stand by for your arrival. Next thing, I get a telex that you're inbound and I'm to bring you and the rest of the crew to Udorn for meetings early tomorrow morning. What gives?"

Looking a bit sheepish—which was not his style at all—Thibodeaux replied, "Sir, I hate to begin our relationship on this note but my answer to your question is to tell you that I hope all will be clear after those meetings tomorrow. At this moment I am not able to discuss the matter further."

Schaffer let out a grunt—actually more like a snort, but from the diaphragm. "Well, it appears you're not cowed by rank or rancor. I guess that's a good thing. Let's get your stuff to your quarters and then meet the crew. I've got Sergeant Williamson standing by with the paperwork signing you into the squadron and certifying you as an aircraft commander per my instructions from Rescue Headquarters. You know, we generally don't do this. I mean, you'd normally be here three weeks to a month, take several training flights and then a special check ride before we'd certify you as an aircraft commander—but I'm under orders. So let's hope you're as good as headquarters says you are."

"Sir," Thibodeaux emphasized the word to make sure the colonel understood that while others might think he was special he did not hold that view of himself. "Sir, like you, I'm under orders. For whatever reason, higher headquarters has chosen me for the mission you'll be briefed on tomorrow and I intend to do my best. I will also do my best to support you and this squadron in any and all assignments you give me."

Schaffer gave another grunting snort. "You'll need your dopp kit and some fresh underwear. I assume you have flight suits with you?"

"Yes sir. I also have a ballistic helmet that was made at Hill Air Force Base by the test squadron personal equipment staff. It's a test version of a new form-fitting helmet where they pour a mold of your head and then make a helmet insert. It's actually much more comfortable than the standard helmets if..."

"If what?" the colonel appeared interested.

"If you always keep your hair cut exactly the same length. Otherwise you get hotspots. So, I guess I'll be making weekly visits to the barber."

Schaffer chuckled. "Well, we have people who do that anyway since the Thai barbers here are women and they give massages with the haircuts." Then, thinking he should clarify, "Scalp massages. You want any other kind of massage you got to go to the Venus in beautiful downtown Nakhon Phanom."

Thibodeaux smiled for even he had heard—as far away as Hill Air Force Base in Utah—about the famous Venus restaurant and massage parlor.

The flight to Udorn that night was no less than a check ride. The colonel even scheduled a C-130 tanker mission near the end of the flight so Thibodeaux could demonstrate his night refueling proficiency. The aircraft crew also ran a night recovery scenario at one of the Rescue training sites between NKP and Udorn. It was during this portion of the flight that Jean-Louis revealed a new piece of technology. Rather than relying solely on the aircraft's low-level light camera display, he used a device he had attached to his new helmet. He explained to the colonel, who rode in the flight engineer's seat of the aircraft, "It's a one-eye night vision device we're experimenting with. It allows me to see outside the cockpit with my right eye while using my left to monitor the aircraft's camera and infrared illuminator. It sucks for depth perception, but its lumens capability is an improvement on the current night vision goggles. Unfortunately, if I use it for more than thirty seconds or so at a time, I'll be on my hands and knees puking my guts out after the mission."

Colonel Schaffer was impressed. Not just with the technology, but with how professionally Thibodeaux handled the aircraft and crew. Thibodeaux fit seamlessly into a situation that had to be stressful. A long flight from Clark in the Philippines, a quick briefing, and immediately into the air in an alien environment. It was apparent that the instructors at Hill AFB had correctly identified something special in this just-promoted captain. "He is good. Very good," the colonel thought. During the refueling exercise, Thibodeaux had driven the fifty-thousand-pound helicopter directly from the pre-contact position into the contact position, putting his refueling probe into the receptacle on the first try. He had done so effortlessly, making the complicated maneuver seem like child's play.

"No, not very good," Schaffer thought, "unparalleled. There isn't a pilot in the squadron who can fly this smoothly. No wonder they want him to do whatever it is we're heading to Udorn to discover."

As Thibodeaux backed off the refueling hose he said to Stretch, "Copilot's airplane. Plug in, take five hundred pounds, disconnect, then drop to nap of the earth altitude and take us to Udorn. Your discretion on approach." Thibodeaux gave Stretch control of the aircraft for Stretch's check ride, monitored by Thibodeaux. He needed to see how well Stretch handled the aircraft at night low level as pilot in command. Thibodeaux said nothing else during the flight except to respond, as the copilot, to Stretch's instructions.

As the rotors wound slowly to a stop, Stretch took his helmet off. He looked across the semi-dark cockpit. "Well?"

"You'll do, but here's the real challenge. You fill out the 781," Thibodeaux said, referring to the aircraft flight log. "I think we'll call it a T-1 night training mission unless the colonel prefers to call it a check ride." He grinned and glanced at the colonel in the half-light provided by the parking ramp's light stanchions. As he looked across the cockpit, the light from one of the stanchions shone into Thibodeaux's eyes and the colonel was struck by the vibrant, emerald-green color of those eyes. They conveyed at once humor and trustworthiness, but there was something much more profound. In that one glance, the colonel was overwhelmed by an almost other-worldliness. Looking into Thibodeaux's eyes, Schaffer felt a surge of confidence suffuse his being.

"Damn!" he thought. "There's something about this guy. He's not just a great pilot. There's something else."

They spent the night in the Udorn Royal Thai Air Force Base Bachelor Officer Quarters.

The meeting room was like every other meeting room in Southeast Asia. Damp, cold from the air-conditioning, and smelling of decaying wood. There were three people present in addition to the military crew that had flown up from NKP. That crew included Schaffer, Thibodeaux, Stretch, the two PJs, and Jésus—the flight engineer. The three additional men were dressed as civilians. One wore a short-sleeved safari jacket over khakis, one wore a short-sleeved white guayabera over khakis, and the third—obviously the Washington presence—wore a long-sleeved white button-down with his sleeves rolled up. He also wore a tie and seersucker trousers, clearly part of a suit, and his jacket was draped over one of the ubiquitous aluminum chairs around the table.

First, the Washington man demanded everyone sign non-disclosure forms and secrecy agreements. The papers promised what seemed like nothing short of death or long-term imprisonment for revealing to anyone outside the room what they were about to hear.

"We have need to place teams of people inside North Vietnam." This from the man in the safari jacket, who looked to be the senior of the three. "We've explored all possible methods of managing these placements and are down to one. Insertion and extraction at night by means of helicopter. None of our helicopters have the range to reach the Chinese border." At this point the man stopped and waited for the phrase "Chinese border" to sink in. "In fact," he continued, "none of our choppers have the range to get much beyond the northern Laotian border without refueling. Since we don't have aerial refueling capabilities we would have to set up remote Lima sites to support the mission, and that would just mean more people and more chance for failure or compromise."

"Uh, sir…" this from Jésus. "What exactly will these teams be doing?"

If looks could have killed, Jésus would have instantly been six feet under given the dagger-like stares immediately thrown at him by all three civilians in the room.

"That is not your concern, Sergeant. All you need be concerned with is getting the teams *to* a particular spot at a particular time or picking them up *from* a specific spot at a specified time. Clear?" Again, it was Safari Jacket who spoke.

"Yes, sir. You call, we haul." Jésus didn't fear authority. After all, he was the best flight engineer in the squadron and they had asked him on this little trip. Still, it seemed like he ought to know what he was risking his life for. He had signed on to rescue people, not fight the war—if that was what this mission entailed.

Not looking happy, Safari Jacket continued, "If you're shot down, you're to destroy your aircraft with thermite charges and make your way south. If you're captured, you don't know anything other than...how was it you put it, Sergeant? You call, we haul? You won't know where the next mission is, so you won't be able to compromise any information other than that we're putting black teams into the country, which we believe they suspect anyway."

He pulled five scarf-sized pieces of silk from a box on the table. The scarves had the US flag and five blocks of five separate languages printed on one side. On the other was a map of North Vietnam, Laos, and Thailand.

"Here are additional blood chits for each of you. In case you don't read Vietnamese, you're now each worth five thousand dollars in gold if delivered alive. So, for God's sake, don't go around wearing baht chains or Rolex watches. That's too much temptation for even some of our loyal tribesmen. You'd think you Air Force types would already know that."

Thibodeaux looked down at the Seiko watch he wore. It had cost fifty bucks in the exchange. No problem there. He made a mental note to check the rest of the crew. He had heard about crewmen who wore gold chains—called baht chains—or expensive watches they planned to use to ransom themselves if they were shot down. It didn't make much sense, because if the tribesmen wanted your expensive Rolex they could just take it and then turn you over to the bad guys, or simply kill you. So far, he agreed with the advice from his friends at the CIA.

"Yes," Thibodeaux thought. "I know they're CIA because I met with them in the United States, but Schaffer and the others don't know—although I expect they suspect such. They should. Who else would come up with these crazy schemes?" Realizing his ruminating was causing him to miss part of Safari Jacket's instructions, he came back into the moment.

"We hope to give you at least twenty-four hours notice before a mission, but if the shit hits the fan, advance notice that your services are required may be much shorter. Questions?"

There weren't many questions to ask. Equipment requirements for the team? They already carried everything they needed. Would they have night vision capability? Limited. How would safety signals be exchanged? Each mission would have a different set, and these would arrive with the courier. This last answered an unspoken question. How would they be notified? A courier from Udorn would arrive with an appropriate flight map, the coordinates of the drop or pick-up, and pertinent information on safety signals for identifying the team to be inserted or extracted.

"Other questions?"

When there were none, Safari Jacket thanked them for coming over and wished them a safe flight back. As they headed for the door he reminded them of the requirement to keep the information secret. He added, "We'll have the first mission ginned up in a couple of weeks. I assume you'll be ready?"

Looking at his men walking out the door, Colonel Schaffer turned back, "Already are." He followed the crew through the door.

The flight back to NKP was primarily a sightseeing excursion as Colonel Schaffer showed Thibodeaux around the local flying area. When they had shut down and made it back to the squadron headquarters building, M.Sgt. Williamson met them with more papers for Thibodeaux to sign. Less than twenty-four hours in country and he had already signed more papers than he could keep track of. He hoped he hadn't signed away his birthright, but then remembered one of the papers was, in fact, an insurance policy acknowledgement. He hoped he had remembered to make his parents his beneficiaries, but then he laughed, because the last people in the world who needed ten thousand additional dollars were his parents.

Finally alone, he found himself standing in a hallway facing the pictures of dead Jolly Green crewmembers. "In Memoriam" the black painted arc above each photo of an Air Rescue crewman said. "All Heroes" the green paint below the photos proclaimed. He looked into the eyes of each of the men pictured in the photographs. He believed that, even after death, you could learn something of the soul of a man by looking at a photograph of his eyes. "This one was afraid," he thought to himself as he looked at the picture of a young lieutenant. "This one should have been afraid," he thought, looking at the photo of one of the squadron's most heroic PJs. "It might have saved his life if he had been."

"It's an all volunteer squadron," he mused aloud. He couldn't help but feel a momentary sense of pride. "All volunteer," he repeated to himself.

At his right shoulder, two first lieutenants appeared from an office marked "Operations Officer." Jean-Louis made a mental note to introduce himself to the ops officer since that officer was number two in charge at the squadron. At the moment though, Jean-Louis was tired and wanted to unpack his duffel and hit the rack for a few hours.

"Excuse me, Captain." It was the taller of the two lieutenants.

Turning, Jean-Louis looked eye-to-eye with the taller, then cut his eyes downward slightly to acknowledge the shorter. "Yes?"

The shorter blurted out, "Is it true you've never been a copilot?"

Jean-Louis saw immediately where this was going, but he played the game. "I'm sorry? Do you mean have I ever been designated as a copilot on the HH-53 helicopter?"

Both had to think a second, but the taller answered. "Yes, that's what we mean. Have you ever been designated a copilot? We ask…" He hesitated briefly, but his mission was clear and he was prepared. "We ask because the squadron only has a few aircraft commander positions and you just took a slot one of the existing copilots might have gotten. Generally, new pilots are designated as copilots, especially first lieutenants or recently promoted captains—" here he coughed just a little, "—like yourself. We sort of get in line with seniority based on service in the squadron and then, when our turn comes, we upgrade and get our own crew. So, we were just wondering how it is you managed to walk in noon yesterday and by today you have your own crew." The lieutenant got bolder as he made his case. He was, after all, the most senior of the junior pilots and next on the list to attempt the upgrade to aircraft commander. The shorter of the two, of course, was second on the list of some thirty-five junior pilots. Both thought that for whatever reason the new crew had been created, the existing promotion order should have been respected. The fact that neither was qualified on Night Recovery Systems—NRS—didn't enter their logic.

In addition to his unique eyes, Jean-Louis possessed an empathic ability that, in many situations, allowed him to understand motivations at a deeper level. Standing in front of him were two senior first lieutenants who knew full well that the squadron commander did not have to abide by any tradition of perceived tribal procession. The squadron commander formed crews based on the mission's needs and his assessment of ability. Knowing that, why would these two confront Jean-Louis?

As he looked first into the eyes of the taller and then the shorter, he understood. This was their attempt to establish that they were the senior copilots and thus forces to be reckoned with.

"Hmmm...let me think on that a moment." Jean-Louis fixed them with his eyes. Both wanted to look away, but could not. Reaching down into his helmet bag, Jean-Louis extracted a pilot's logbook which he handed to the taller one.

"Here's my log book. At the back is a summary of types of aircraft I have flown and the pilot ratings I possess. For example, I'm a civilian Certified Flight Instructor. I have an Air Transport Pilot rating in non-centerline thrust aircraft. And—oh, yes—I've flown fighters. Not for long, but long enough. Now, to answer your question. No, I have never been a copilot on the HH-53, but I have lots of hours as a copilot in L-19 Beavers, DC-3s and Lear jets—so let's just say I've done my time in the other seat. Read the log. Share it around the squadron if you want. Just don't lose it."

It was obvious that with the log he was dismissing them. They left, but quickly sought out Stretch.

"Man, don't you hate it that you're not going to get your own crew?" The taller one still had to look up significantly to catch Stretch's eyes.

In his trademark laconic manner Stretch considered before answering. "Look guys, I'm not as into the move-up program as you two. For me, mission is the important thing, and, having flown twice now with Captain Thibodeaux, I can tell you I think I'm going to be in on a lot of interesting flights. Besides, if last night and this morning were any indication, I'm going to be flying the aircraft at least half the time anyway. Out of the four hours we've already flown together I have almost two hours of pilot-in-command time. Do your aircraft commanders allow you to fly half the time and log it? Last night we hit a tanker between here and Udorn and after he plugged in and disconnected Thibodeaux made me do it from the left seat. How many times do you get to plug into a completely dark C-130?"

"Okay, Okay. We get it," the taller one gave in. "So what call sign do we give your new commander?"

Here the shorter one chimed in. "That stateside red, white, and blue nametag he has on his flight suit…. it's very Captain America so how about that, 'Captain America'? We haven't had a Captain America in a long time."

The taller lieutenant looked like he was about to agree when Stretch said, "Call him what you want, but his crew is just going to call him 'the Captain.'"

"You mean like, 'The Captain and Tenille'?" The shorter one almost giggled. However, since it was very unbecoming for a combat pilot to giggle, he managed to choke it back.

"No," Stretch expanded. "Like '*the* Captain.' You watch. I'll bet you Schaffer makes him the assistant operations officer."

"No way!" The taller was incredulous. "He's much too junior. It'll piss off all the other captains in the squadron."

Stretch, standing up straight so that his pronouncement came from on high, predicted, "Not when they've met him it won't. Mark my words gentlemen, he's a unique person, and before long you'll just be referring to him as 'the Captain'."

Boots under his bunk, flight suit off, Jean-Louis lay down on the somewhat damp sheets. It was time to break out the heating pad he had in his duffel bag. If he left the heating pad on low and tucked it between the sheets when he wasn't in the room, the sheets would be dry when he climbed into them. Still, these sheets weren't the starched and ironed heavy sheets he had grown up sleeping on. Sheets that had resisted the dampness and wetness enough so they didn't bunch up around you when you climbed into bed. But, even though these sheets were much thinner, the heating pad would help.

As he felt sleep taking him to another place, he thought, "We may be heroes in waiting when we're in the air, but on the ground we're just like every other squadron. Sometimes petty, almost humorously so. Still, in the air everyone lives by the Rescue motto, 'That Others May Live'." He smiled as he floated into a sound sleep. He always slept soundly, damp sheets or not.

Not quite two weeks after their Udorn meeting, a courier arrived. When they plotted out the coordinates for the drop-off point on their maps it was so close to the Chinese border that Jean-Louis knew he would have to bang the tree tops off the bottom of the aircraft just to stay under the Chinese radar. "Well," he commented to the crew as they studied the map, "there goes another Doppler radar housing."

CHAPTER 2

ONE ROUND, TWO PURPLE HEARTS

THE WESTERN HORIZON CLUNG TO its purplish hue, seemingly loath to leave the approaching helicopter alone in the dark. Silhouetted against that dark purple, the aircraft appeared black and somber, appropriate for its mission. It was returning the body of its pilot, and was being flown by its wounded copilot. The crowd gathered on the flight line was not unlike a group of mourners at a graveside awaiting the arrival of the hearse. No one spoke. They just watched as the silhouette grew larger. Even the sounds of the flight line seemed somehow subdued. Other aircraft were being held in place on the airdrome while the Jolly Green approached.

The landing approach was uneven—stair-stepped like an uncertain pilot-in-training—but finally the bird was on the ground and immediately surrounded by ambulances, fire engines, and maintenance vans. The medics went on board first, but the copilot refused to let them bring him out on a stretcher. He was helped out of his seat by his own two PJs. He had some trouble clearing the radio console that separated his seat from the pilot's, but the PJs steadied him over it and down the two steps into the cargo compartment. Then they helped him out of the crew door. One of the PJs held up the copilot's right hand. It was bandaged from the elbow down to the middle of the palm. There was still wet blood on the copilot's sleeve and all the way down the front of his flight suit.

Out of the aircraft and no longer in command, the copilot continued to resist the medics' efforts to put him in an ambulance. He insisted on waiting until they had removed the body of his aircraft commander.

Thibodeaux admired the loyalty but wondered to himself how much was occasioned by an overabundance of adrenaline and a loss of blood that slowed the thinking process.

The two PJs, with the assistance of some of the medics, brought the body bag containing the remains of Captain Jon B. Coldman from the aircraft. The PJs had removed his body from the pilot's seat and placed it in a body bag shortly after he had been shot. The flight engineer had then flipped the bloody cushion over and climbed into the pilot's seat to assist the copilot in flying the aircraft. Some aircraft commanders made sure their flight engineers could make basic flight movements at the controls of the aircraft. Captain Coldman had been one of those aircraft commanders. And so the flight engineer had held the helicopter in steady flight while the PJs attended to the copilot, bandaging his arm and splinting his wrist.

As they moved the body bag to a waiting ambulance, all those on the ramp came to attention and saluted. The young copilot attempted to bring his right arm into a salute, but, as he did so, the draining adrenaline level and the loss of blood finally induced the shock he had fought off for three-quarters of an hour. It overcame him, and he slumped into the arms of the two medics who, having taken him from the PJs, had steadied him. They placed him on a gurney and into one of the waiting ambulances. As they did so, Thibodeaux walked over and asked, "What's his blood type, and do you have enough in the clinic?"

One of the medics unzipped the top part of the copilot's flight suit and dug under his T-shirt for the dog tags. "O," he pronounced, "We should be fine. Won't need any donors." Thibodeaux stepped back. The doors closed and the ambulance headed for the clinic.

As the assistant operations officer, Thibodeaux would have to write the combat report for this flight since neither the pilot nor copilot would be able. Thibodeaux would also make notes during the intelligence debrief of the flight engineer and the PJs, and during the separate debriefs of the A-1 Skyraider "Sandy" aircraft pilots when they returned—which should be shortly since they, in their standard rescue role, were escorting Jolly Green 32 on its return to base. Jolly 32 had made the rescue Captain Coldman's crew was originally attempting when he was killed.

Yet another ambulance arrived from the clinic and the fire trucks remained on standby although the second rescue attempt had gone without incident. Jolly 32's battle damage report was a clean "negative damage."

Ordinarily there would have been a great fanfare as there was for every successful rescue, but today the atmosphere was subdued and the arrival of the survivor aboard Jolly 32 was handled almost as if it was an everyday event. The survivor was assisted out of the helicopter by the PJs, transferred to an ambulance, and spirited away for a medical exam by flight surgeons at the clinic.

The champagne bottles normally passed around by those celebrating the rescue remained corked. The pilot and copilot of Jolly 32 asked after the crew of Jolly 41 and were told that Captain Coldman had been killed. They knew this, of course, because Jolly 41's copilot's initial radio transmission had been, "Uhhhhh, Jolly Green 41 is breaking off our run-in. We just lost our pilot." Later, during the debrief, Jolly 41's flight engineer and PJs confirmed that transmission, as did the Sandy pilots in their separate session with the intelligence officers. Sandy Lead told this story:

"We had identified the position of the survivor. He'd parachuted into an area near the base of a ridge that, according to our maps, was at three thousand feet above sea level and just over two thousand feet above the surrounding terrain. We drug the area for enemy fire. Receiving no fire and seeing no hostiles in the immediate area, we cleared Jolly 41 for a rescue run-in attempt. Sandy 2 led him down towards the survivor who popped an orange smoke canister upon request. The Jolly was flying parallel to the right of the ridgeline during his descent, and when he was about 1,800 feet AGL—above ground level—the copilot told us they were breaking off their approach because they had just lost their pilot."

The other three Sandy pilots confirmed the narration with nods of their heads as Sandy Lead continued to describe the events.

"I asked Jolly 41 where the ground fire had originated and his response seemed a little disoriented. After seeing how much blood there was in the cockpit of the aircraft, I can understand why." Sandy Lead stopped his story long enough to wipe his forehead and scratch his nose with the back of his hand. These were, it appeared to the others, just attempts to wipe the tears from his eyes without appearing to do so. He continued:

"The Jolly kept saying the ground fire must have come from three o'clock because the pilot was hit in the head. That's the pilot's side of the aircraft, so we asked two or three times more because it seemed unlikely someone shooting from almost directly below the aircraft at that angle could have hit the pilot in the head. Just as I was about to ask again, I heard the copilot say, 'No....wait...the ground fire must have come from nine o'clock because I'm hit, too.'

"At that point we had to assume that someone, firing from the ridge line, had fired down at the Jolly. The round must have gone through the plexiglass of the copilot's window, struck the copilot in the forearm, and then the pilot in the head. We didn't see how this could have happened, but on the way over here I spoke with the copilot of Jolly 32 and he told me that one of the jobs of the copilot during a combat run-in is to guard the overhead throttles from slipping backwards, so Jolly 41's copilot's right arm would have been up on the throttle quadrant. That picture makes sense."

Sandy Lead went on to explain how Jolly 41 had turned away from the area and headed home. The necessary radio calls were made and King Bird—the rescue control aircraft—asked for a backup Jolly to be launched and to intercept Jolly 41 on his way home. Then, rather than sweep the area looking for a single lucky rifleman, Sandy had changed the approach direction and brought Jolly 32 in via a different route. The remainder of the rescue had gone without incident. The backup rescue aircraft had intercepted Jolly 41, but 41's copilot assured them he could make it back to base so the backup aircraft loitered between the rescue site and 41's flight path home—ready to assist either Jolly 41 or Jolly 32 if required.

Thibodeaux had what he needed and, in his office, set about typing the report of the death of Captain Coldman. It was a simple report that required no more investigation. There was no indication of any wrongdoing on anyone's part. He had confirmed that there was a single hole in the plexiglass copilot's side window of Jolly 41. Since the window unit was easy to replace, the aircraft would be returned to duty in short order. The single largest maintenance challenge would be cleaning the blood splatter from the instrument panel and elsewhere in the cockpit. Thibodeaux did not know for sure, but he was reasonably certain that whoever flew Jolly 41 for the foreseeable future would smell and taste the iron and rust flavored bouquet of dried blood, especially when they sat on the ramp in the 120-degree heat.

He typed the last period, signed the report, placed it in an envelope, and dropped it in the squadron commander's inbox for his endorsement.

As Thibodeaux pushed through the doors of the Jolly Green Bar he noted that the establishment had not taken on the atmosphere of either an Irish wake or a Southern Baptist viewing at a funeral home. It remained just a bar. There were people playing poker at one table while others sat at other tables or the bar, drinks in front of them. Four young lieutenants plied a pinball machine that was older than any of them. Although it did not appear to be a place honoring a death in the family, Thibodeaux could read the signs. The bets at the poker table were not as aggressive as they should have been and the *bonhomie* at the pinball machine was forced. The drinkers sat with their unfinished drinks on the bar or table, not in their hands. They contemplated something, and it was not difficult to know what. They were thinking, he knew, not of death in the abstract, nor of the death of Captain Coldman, but of their own potential deaths.

This was not good. One of the more senior officers needed to redirect the thought in this place, but Thibodeaux knew he should not be the one to do so. Even though he was the assistant operations officer, there were too many who resented his elevation both to aircraft commander and to the number three position in the squadron. This situation needed leadership, but not his. He ordered a Jim Beam, straight up.

More officers joined those in the bar, coming from their respective duties. Stretch crouched a little to clear the doorjamb. Like the others, he did not remove his green baseball cap, thus adding to what appeared to be a swelling sea of green caps in the large room. He stood next to Thibodeaux at the bar and ordered, "Scotch, rocks."

"Stretch…" Thibodeaux leaned forward toward the bar and right toward Stretch. "Stretch, if somebody doesn't do something these guys are going to eat their insides out thinking about dying." Stretch looked around the room. His assessment confirmed his aircraft commander's. The appearance of normalcy was a fiction. He also sensed and understood Thibodeaux's reluctance to act.

"So, what do you think, boss?" he asked, not having to lift his voice to be heard because other than the pinging of the pinball machine the room was quiet.

"A toast. Offer a toast to Coldman." Thibodeaux was firm. "We've got to get them talking about something they can focus on other than their own deaths."

At this, Stretch pushed himself up on the foot rail of the bar, rising to a commanding height in the room. "Gentlemen of the Squadron," he spoke sonorously. "A toast to a fallen comrade." He had their attention. People turned, chairs shuffled. They all stood, glasses in their hands. "To Captain Jon Coldman, a true Jolly Green. He died that others might live." Stretch raised his glass and all and sundry followed suit. He drank.

One of the lieutenants near the pinball machine blurted, "May his death help end this senseless war. He died for his country."

A captain at the poker table spoke. "That's bullshit! Patton was right when he said no bastard ever won a war by dying for his country...and this isn't even a fucking war." This declaration brought cheers of "damn straight" and "fucking 'A'."

Another captain across the poker table added, "Right. All we're doing is...what was it Johnson said? 'Sending a message to the Vietnamese.' We're fucking messengers, like those guys that ride the bicycles in New York. Nobody cares if we die." This pronouncement also brought loud murmurs and shouts of assent.

Others joined in, their rancor concentrated on the generals and politicians who did not face death. More anger was directed at those people in the streets at home who avoided service and accused the pilots and crews in Southeast Asia of being war criminals.

"Now they're thinking of anger, not death," Thibodeaux murmured to Stretch. He looked around for someone to take that anger and channel it, to use it as a binding agent to bring cohesion. But no one moved. The squadron commander and the operations officer were not in the bar. None of the senior captains, including those who had just spoken, said anything else. If no one seized the moment, within minutes the silence would return and everyone would, once again, return to fearing their own deaths.

Thibodeaux thought about making a speech from the top of the bar in the manner of Henry the Fifth. "We few, we happy few, we band of brothers..." sort of thing, but he instinctively knew that would be too much. It would invite derision from his numerous detractors and that would shut down the chance of finding some much-needed military cohesion.

Instead, he moved to the old Baldwin upright piano that sat next to the pinball machine. It was out of tune from the constant humidity, but it was a consistent out-of-tune that allowed each string to vibrate with a resonance appropriate in value to the next string up or down. So if he transposed a bit he could play a song reasonably well.

He struck up the tune and sang:

> *"Stand to your glasses, laddies,*
> *Don't let a tear fill your eye,*
> *Here's to the dead and ready,*
> *Hurrah for the next man to die!*
> *For we are the boys who fly high in the sky,*
> *Losing buddies while boozing are we,*
> *We are the ones who they send out to die..."*

Here he stopped, his hands on the keys. His strong tenor voice resonated:

"Some call us criminals and, in a sense we are, for every day we rob Death of his due. We look into that dark, cowl-covered visage, into those hollow sockets, and we tell him, 'Not today!' No gentlemen, we do not deliver death, rather we deliver *from* death, and in order to do so, each of us is prepared to die. We are willing to pay the toll on Charon's ferry to permit another soul to stay on this side of the river Styx."

He played and sang, his tenor so right for the song:

> *"Up at headquarters they scream and they shout,*
> *Shouting of things they know nothing about..."*

He stopped again, hands still on the keys.

"Yes, there are those who do not understand what we do, but we know. And those who fly in this war know, that if required, we will come for them. And, gentlemen, that is all that is necessary."

He played:

"For we are the boys who fly high in the sky,
Losing buddies while boozing are we..."

He stopped playing and concluded:

"Whether this is a war, whether it is a legal war, whether young cowards in the States burn their draft cards or their bras is not our concern. We are a brotherhood dedicated to a single cause. Death shall not win even if we have to offer ourselves in the place of others. Now everybody!"

He played, once more:

"Stand to your glasses, laddies.
Don't let a tear fill your eye,
Here's to the dead and ready..."

He brought the piano to its loudest to be heard over voices now loud enough to rattle the shoddily installed glass window panes:

"HURRAH *for the next man to die!"*

Before the vibration of the strings could die or the voices be stilled, he launched into:

"JOLLY GREEN, JOLLY GREEN,
Prettiest sight that I've ever seen..."

And those present sang the squadron song with gusto, once again filled with confidence. There was true camaraderie in their singing. Again they were a cohesive unit, each part of the whole, focused on a common mission and no longer, at least for the moment, worried that they might be that next man.

CHAPTER 3

FIND YOUR OWN WAY HOME

THEIR STOMACH AND SPHINCTER MUSCLES had relaxed enough to allow them to swallow the nausea of fear, but not enough to provide the total relief that would have eased their white knuckles, cramped necks, and tense shoulders. In truth, total relief would never come, for adrenalin always coursed through their bodies whether they were in the air or sitting through the long hours of alert. They could slow the adrenalin with alcohol in the evening, but it would be there when they woke in the morning. It always was.

It had been pretty much a textbook operation. Vampire 32 had exploded just north of the Ho Chi Minh Trail and the pilot had parachuted into some trees a few miles inside North Vietnam. Inbound to the rescue site, Thibodeaux and Stretch had discussed the poor pilots who had to fly the Vampire aircraft. Vampires were just push-pull civilian Cessnas, with superchargers that allowed them to fly at twenty thousand feet.

The airplanes were crammed with radios and acted as orbiting relay stations for a variety of otherwise line of sight radio nets. Flying a Vampire was probably the dullest pilot mission in the entire theater of conflict. Dull, that is, until the supercharger broke a belt, and the engine—starved for air—exploded. Then the pilot had little choice but to allow himself to free fall to an altitude below ten thousand feet and deploy his parachute.

Thus it was they found Vampire 32 hanging by the risers of his chute almost a hundred feet off the ground and unable to deploy his "get down" harness because his arm had been broken by crashing through the upper limbs of the very tall trees he had encountered during his descent. Many of those same upper limbs were themselves broken and bent beyond repair in their own turn when Thibodeaux's fifty-thousand-pound helicopter settled over the top of the tree, the ninety-plus-mile-an-hour downwash from its massive rotor pounding the branches with the power of a category two hurricane.

"Right three...two...one...stop...hold your hover...you're going too far...left one...stop...hold your hover...PJ is going down...hold your hover...right one...stop...hold your hover... you're too high...down two...PJ is next to survivor...hold your hover...down one...down one...stop...you're sliding right... left two...left one...stop...hold your hover...PJ is attaching line to his harness...hold your hover...you're sliding left to right... dammit Jean-Louis hold your hover...PJ is cutting loose risers...hold your hover...PJ has survivor clear the tree...lifting hoist line..." Jésus gave precise instructions and Thibodeaux flew the giant helicopter with the touch of a surgeon excising a tumor from deep within the brain of his patient—even if it did not seem so to the flight engineer who was hanging out the door operating the rescue hoist.

"Survivor and PJ twenty feet below the aircraft...hold your hover...ten feet...hold your hover...Survivor coming in the door...survivor and PJ in the aircraft...door closed, cleared for forward flight." Jésus finished his directions and Thibodeaux pushed the nose down and pulled up on the collective to transition the large platform from a wind generator once again into a flying machine.

The pilot of Vampire 32 was installed in one of the litters mounted on the sidewall of the cargo bay of the helicopter and ministered to by one of the PJs while the other PJ maintained his position in the gun tub on the ramp of the aircraft. The PJ applied a field cast to 32's arm and hung a drip bag of saline, dextrose, and morphine from the aircraft frame above the stretcher. The morphine dulled the pain of his arm and took 32 to a much better place in his mind than the back of an HH-53 smelling of jet fuel, engine oil, and hydraulic fluid.

Up front, Jésus, Stretch, and Thibodeaux went about their flying duties to recover the aircraft to Nakhon Phanom.

There had been no call for the Sandy support fighters to intervene because no opposition had been detected. The Sandys had simply circled overhead during the rescue ready to claw and rend those who might challenge the humanitarian mission to return Vampire 32 to the bosom of his colleagues and his usual stool at the Vampire bar. Not needed, they still kept station with the two Jolly Greens as they made their way toward the border of North Vietnam and Laos. Two A-1s to the right and slightly above, and two to the left of the formation, with Thibodeaux in back and his high bird, Jolly Green 53—flown by Captain Hiram B. Jolly's crew—leading the formation.

"Christmas couldn't have made that save." Stretch used Captain Jolly's call sign.

"Of course he could have." Thibodeaux was feeling magnanimous. "I think any aircraft commander in the squadron and the majority of the copilots could have done that as easily as I did."

Stretch, not to be denied his assertion, answered, "Nope. Almost all those guys would have blown the pilot out of the tree with the downwash. Nobody else would have hovered that far above the trees. They would have gone lower, and in doing so would have thrashed 32 in the trees with the rotor wash." Stretch explained his reasoning.

Thibodeaux looked across the cockpit at his sometimes-too-loyal copilot, "I say any other aircraft commander would have done as well. By the way, copilot's airplane. Take us home." He shook the stick as Stretch took control of the aircraft.

"My airplane," Stretch announced, following protocol and also shaking the stick lightly to indicate he was now flying the airplane, "but, NO WAY, José ! No other pilot could've got 32 out without messing him up more than he was already from the bailout and hitting the trees."

"Did somebody invite me to the conversation?" It was Jésus.

Thibodeaux looked back over his left shoulder at the diminutive flight engineer. "Nope. He said "José, not Jésus."

Raising the dark visor on his helmet, Jésus looked at Thibodeaux. "Well, I thought he might just have gotten my name wrong. After all, these tall guys don't think that fast. You know…it's because of how long it takes to get the blood from their hearts to their brains." He grinned and seemed about to ask something when Stretch cut him off.

"And you don't think I didn't see…wait, is that a double negative? Anyway, I saw you doing that little dance in the air. You put the rotor up a little to the left, then rotor up a little to the right, then kicked the pedal just slightly. You were spilling air from under our rotors to make the downwash less violent. That's why Jésus was so exasperated. Left here, right there… up…no, down…You're almost always rock steady but today you danced the airplane through a box step, spilling a little air here and a little air there. Did it ever occur to you we were already hovering at maximum out-of-ground effect altitude for the elevation, weight, and temperature? Of course it did, but you knew exactly what you were doing, didn't you? And I still say that no one else in the squadron could have made that rescue and done it in four minutes either." Stretch was exercised.

Jésus reached out and punched Thibodeaux in the upper arm. "There I was thinking you were nursing some kind of hangover, or had come down with some nerve disease, or were having a stroke—and all the time you're dancing the airplane on purpose. I swear, Captain…I never know what white guys like you are going to do."

"Hold on there, Jésus." This from Stretch. "What do you mean, 'white guys like you'? Our intrepid aircraft commander is, I believe, what is officially known as a Cajun. Brother to the alligator and water moccasin. Eater of mudbugs and other such bayou delicacies."

Thibodeaux had drawn his right knee up toward his chest and had his boot on the instrument panel in an effort to forestall the leg and lower back cramps that often followed extensively tense hovering episodes.

"Stretch, what on earth did they teach you at the academy? I'm not really a full blood Cajun. I'm French, Scots-Irish, and American Indian. My grandmother is a Choctaw Indian whose father was part Acadian. That I was born in the bayou does not automatically make me a Cajun, nor does having a French name—but I love the fact that I can sound pretty authentic when I need to." And here he dropped into a thick Acadian accent.

"Besides *mon frère*, if you never chowed down on boiled crawdads you have no concept of what it will be like in heaven. *Mon Dieu*, I'm needing me some boiled crawfish and cold beer right now." He changed legs and dropped the accent. "So, I'm a little bit Acadian and a whole lot of other things. But mostly I'm just American.

"In fact, the more I think about it, the more I think we'll repair to the bar when we land. I do believe they'll have some of that cold beer there—even if they haven't got the crawfish. After debrief, of course."

"Well, after that piece of flying I bet you won't have any trouble getting guys to buy you a drink …just in hopes you'll share your technique." Jésus noted this because he knew he would be at Jean-Louis' elbow throughout the coming evening and would be inviting himself in on the proffered drinks—since he would be the self-designated "nodder." That is, Jean-Louis would say something and Jésus would nod his head up and down, assuring others that it was so.

"Say, if you're part Choctaw do you have a Choctaw name?" This from Stretch, who was obviously searching for pun material.

"Do you mean do I have a name they call me when I go up to visit my grandmother on the reservation? Something like that?" Thibodeaux saw what was coming.

"Yeah. What do they call you on the reservation? That's exactly what I mean."

"Well, mostly they call me Jean-Louis but sometimes they just yell, 'Hey You!'"

Stretch was defeated in his effort.

After a moment's thought, Thibodeaux turned to Jésus. "No, I don't think we'll say anything about spilling air or high hover. In fact, Jésus, reach down here and unplug the voice recorder. No, hang on. Run it back to about ten minutes into the flight and erase all after that. Last thing we want is some after action flight evaluator—you know, like the Blue Meanie—listening to all this chatter. I mean, 'high hover,' 'spilling,' and all this too-familiar banter must be against somebody's rules and regulations, and we certainly don't want to have to put up with the Blue Meanie on an unscheduled check ride."

Jésus did as instructed.

Having stretched both legs and his back as much as possible in the confines of the aircraft's exceedingly uncomfortable seat while wearing the harness of a fifty-pound parachute, Thibodeaux placed his legs back under the instrument panel.

"So, is Christmas on track?" He asked about Jolly Green 53's compass heading towards NKP.

"I'd fly a little more to the south, but I think he doesn't want to fly over the tall karst formations down there." Stretch was nonchalant in his answer.

"Ok, I'll probably be sorry for asking this, but how did you guys decide to give him the call sign 'Christmas?'" Thibodeaux was glad to be somewhat relaxed.

Stretch grinned broadly as he looked across the cockpit. "Oh, come on Jean-Louis, how could we not? I mean the guy's name *is* 'Jolly,' as in 'Jolly ole Saint Nick' or 'A Holly Jolly Christmas.'"

Thibodeaux's smile showed he understood, but he pushed on. "Yeah, but then you had to give that new copilot the call sign 'Elf.' What is that about? Christmas and Elf?" Here he shook his head as if he were perplexed.

Stretch, looking as exasperated as one could from behind a heavily darkened helmet visor answered, "Again, Captain, how could we not? Come on, admit it, he looks like an elf, and Christmas plus Elf is just too good to pass up."

"MiGs! MiGs! MiGs!" The PJ in the gun tub at the rear of the airplane yelled over the interphone. His voice was two octaves higher than his normal baritone Texas drawl.

"MiGs! Six o'clock high!"

Thibodeaux adjusted the mirror he used to see behind him. Sure enough, there were two dark silhouettes against the sky. He keyed his mike, "Sandy Lead, two MiGs, six o'clock high."

Heads in all four of the accompanying Skyraiders whipped around, and the crew on Jolly 53 began to search the sky.

"Sandy Lead to flight. Descend now. Get in the trees. Get in the trees." The voice was raspy but not hurried.

All six aircraft pushed over and headed for the jungle canopy some four thousand feet below them.

"Mayday! Mayday! Mayday! This is Sandy 1-1. Rescue flight of six. Location Crab 22. I say again Crab 22. We have two MiGs. I say again two MiGs." Sandy Lead radioed for help using the emergency communications Guard channel, which all aircraft monitored.

"Sandy 1-1, King 34. Understand MiGs. Crab 22. Joker is being notified." The rescue support C-130 responded to the call.

As the six aircraft headed for the trees, Sandy Lead spoke to the flight, "Get down and bounce the trees off your bellies. We're up sun they may not have spotted us."

"Sandy Lead, this is Sandy 4." The radio amplified the ambient sounds of multiple engines. "No such luck. They just went tactical."

Thibodeaux saw the two MiGs separate themselves by about five hundred feet. He watched as they began to descend on a flight path directly behind the rescue formation. Since Thibodeaux was the last aircraft in the flight he would be the easiest target. Now that the MiGs had separated, their silhouettes were easier to identify. MiG 19s. "Damn!" he thought. Third generation jets. Only the best North Vietnamese pilots and Russian instructors flew these aircraft. They carried three thirty-millimeter cannon as well as air-to-air missiles.

"Sandy Lead to Sandy 2. Take the Jollys home." As he said this, Sandy Lead pulled up and out of the formation in a climbing turn. As the pilot pushed his throttle forward his eighteen-cylinder Curtis Wright radial engine roared belligerently and the four-bladed prop began dragging the heavy airplane upwards and around, towards the descending MiGs.

"Sandy 3, Sandy 2. Get the helicopters back to NKP." This as Sandy Lead's wingman advanced the throttle on his aircraft and followed Sandy Lead's climbing turn.

"Sandy 4, Sandy 3. Your flight, Bubba." He too, followed Lead's arcing climb, his engine adding to the thunderous throb.

"Hell, you can't live forever. Jollys, find your own way home." This from Sandy 4 as he followed his element lead, shoving his throttle forward, while pulling backward and hard to the right on his stick.

Thus, four World War II dive bombers, their thirty-year-old engines and four-bladed props pounding out a rhythmic, almost tribal, beat, rolled out abreast in a line of determined defiance.

"Arm all weapons," Sandy Lead instructed calmly. "Select ripple fire for the rockets. We'll put a wall of lead in front of them and let them fly through it. Separate yourselves by fifty feet in altitude, One high, Two low. Two and I will take the MiG on the left. Three and Four, you get the one on the right. Fire in front of them. Remember, these guys have cannon. Good luck."

Four aircraft that were older than any of the pilots who flew them prepared to do battle with third generation jets flown, most likely, by experienced Russian pilots. Death would surely ensue, but it would be a glorious death. Their story would live on. But now there was nothing glorious. All they felt was fear.

Thibodeaux saw them first. Rather he sensed them—for they approached out of the sun, their shadows rippling across the jungle tops in advance of the actual aircraft. Four US Air Force F-4Es. Then he heard them, their afterburners exploding the very air in which they flew. MiG-Killers!!

"Gun Fighter 22. Flight, go tactical." The radio snapped to life. The four supersonic fighters split into two elements. Just as Sandy Lead had instructed his flight, the lead F-4 very calmly informed his flight. "Two and I will take the MiG on the left. Three and Four, you have the one on the right." As the F-4s passed over the A-1s Thibodeaux heard, "Sandy Lead, sorry to spoil your chance to dance but please allow us to cut in."

The MiGs, seeing the black smoke that trailed the F-4s, had begun diving turns away from the US aircraft. Halfway through their turns they lit their afterburners, the two solid thuds being quickly over taken by the combined roar of jet and radial engines.

Once again, the stomach and sphincter muscles relaxed. Once again, the nausea of not just possible, but probable, death was swallowed. Once again, jaws tensed tight enough to break teeth could return to telling jokes.

On the ground, Thibodeaux did not have to worry about the Blue Meanie discovering his penchant to dance the aircraft or hear the extraneous comments in the cockpit, for the story that day was the heroism of the Sandy pilots, as well it should have been. So the debrief was short and the crew spent the evening in the Jolly Green bar toasting first the Sandys, then the Gunfighters, then the Sandys...and so on, and so on.

CHAPTER 4

WHO BARFS FIRST?

"OUR PASSENGERS NICE AND SNUG in the back?" Thibodeaux turned his head to the left to look into the rear of the aircraft.

Jésus, stepping up on the gun box and thus blocking his captain's view, replied. "All belted in, and I gave them all headsets so you can talk to them directly. In fact, they're listening to us now on intercom." Jésus' transmission carried the background noise of the engines from the cargo compartment of the big aircraft. Since the engines were directly overhead, they were louder in back than on the flight deck where Thibodeaux and Stretch sat.

Once up on the gun box, Jésus leaned into the flight deck and circumvented the intercom by shouting directly into Jean-Louis' ear. "Jesus Christ, Jean-Louis. There's a woman with them this time. She looks like she's Vietnamese. And we've got two motorbikes strapped down."

The pilot leaned in close to Jésus' face and replied in a loud voice, "Don't worry about it. We just fly them in and out. Who they are and what they do is not our concern."

Then, keying the intercom button, he announced, "Good evening, people. This is the captain speaking. Glad to have you with us. If you have an inflight meal box with you I suggest you eat now because once we go low level it tends to get bumpy and, during our refueling, you'll notice a very strong odor of jet fuel that, truthfully, doesn't mix well with chicken salad sandwiches. Especially if the chicken salad has onions in it.

"If you haven't cinched your seat belt real tight across your hips, I suggest you do so now. I know I don't have to tell you how to do your job, but please, no lights of any kind while we're in flight. This is a black mission and we have to remain totally black even though you may sometimes see some red light coming from the cockpit. So, if you're planning to eat, I hope you're good at telling a pickle from a boiled egg by touch. One last thing. If you don't have an air sickness bag readily available, those cardboard inflight dinner boxes work really well and, in fact, hold more than the bags. So I'd keep them handy." Thibodeaux leaned back into the cockpit and, waving his left hand at Stretch, asked for the black ops checklist.

Before Stretch could start with the checklist, Thibodeaux heard a voice on the intercom in Vietnamese. Jean-Louis spoke some Thai and a smattering of Vietnamese that he'd learned in case he had to bail out or was forced down in North Vietnam, but he didn't understand what was being said until he heard the words, "chicken salad." Apparently someone in the back didn't speak English and his instructions were being translated. He wondered if it was the woman. He waited for the translation to be finished and then once again asked for the black ops checklist.

"Star and bar placards removed and stowed?" Stretch asked, referring to the placards on the sides of the aircraft that identified it as a USAF aircraft. Most aircraft had their star and bar insignia painted on, but Jolly 47 did not. Like all the NRS aircraft, its insignia were painted on placards that slipped into and out of brackets mounted to each side of the aircraft.

"Removed and stowed," Jésus replied.

"Window curtains closed?"

"Closed."

"Covers off low level light television camera and infrared illuminator?"

"Covers off."

As Stretch and Jésus went through the checklist, Jean-Louis ran his eyes up and down his aircraft performance gauges and determined that, for the moment, everything was just fine with Jolly 47's systems.

After takeoff he called for the gear-down checklist. Although he got better gas mileage and less vibration with the gear up, he wanted the gear down because after he refueled, the flight profile called for low-level, nap-of-the-earth flying, and he didn't want to have to wait on a gear transit if he had to put the aircraft down in a hurry. Still, with the landing gear down he had to be careful not to snag large branches. Such an occurrence could ruin the entire evening. He climbed the aircraft to four thousand feet, headed for the designated refueling coordinates and, after fifteen minutes, called for the tanker.

"King 33, Jolly 47 ready for training night refueling exercise."

The big C-130 replied, "Jolly 47, King 33. We're looking for you."

"Oh, shit!" It was Stretch. "We've got the rotating beacons off. That's the problem with doing the black ops checklist before we refuel." He reached over and turned the Grimes lights on. The Jolly began to blink red lights from the top of its tail and the bottom of the airplane.

"Tally Ho," King called. "You must've been in a cloud. We're at your five o'clock moving into position."

"In a cloud!" Stretch laughed, "Yeah, in a cloud. That's our story and we're sticking to it." Nobody on the C-130 thought this was anything other than a routine training mission for the night flyers in the helicopter squadron. Then....

"Jolly 47, King. We have a problem with our left hose. Can you take a right hose refueling?"

If faces could have been seen, in both aircraft those of the pilots would have reflected concern while those of each crewmember would have reflected the image from Edvard Munch's painting "The Scream."

Right hose refuelings were bad enough during the daytime, but nobody in their right mind wanted to do a right hose at night. Prop wash from all four of the C-130 engines funneled into a vortex just behind the right wing that housed the refueling hose. This meant the refueling basket attached to the end of the hose moved erratically. Moreover, the air behind and under the wing of the C-130 was extremely turbulent. The turbulence could move the fifty-thousand-pound helicopter up and down and left and right, throwing it about like a balsa wood airplane caught in the vortex of a dust devil. And if that wasn't bad enough, the rotors of the helicopter were ten feet closer to the C-130's horizontal stabilizer and fuselage. No, no sane person wanted to take a right hose at night. Still, the flying safety gurus all agreed that a normally skilled pilot could do it if he was very cautious.

On a normal training mission a sensible aircraft commander would simply write off the refueling part of the exercise, citing equipment problems. Nobody would fault him for not taking a right hose at night, especially since he wasn't supposed to need the fuel to complete the training mission profile he was flying. But Thidodeaux and his crew needed the gas. They couldn't fly an hour over Laos, then an hour into North Vietnam, and then two hours back without replacing the fuel they had already expended flying south to pick up the insertion team at an old abandoned airfield. The aircraft had a significant fuel capacity, especially with its 450-gallon wing tanks, but that still only gave it a four-and-a-half-hour range. Even if everything worked exactly right, they would still be over an hour short of fuel. So, Thibodeaux answered, "King, Jolly. No problem. Let me know when we're cleared into the pre-contact position."

The "Os" on the faces of all the crewmembers, both in the C-130 and in the HH-53, became more pronounced. The PJs on the helicopter edged their way to the ramp at the back of the aircraft. They would hold on to the airframe, ready to step into space if there was contact between the two aircraft. As they moved, they guiltily considered their poor passengers. Each PJ tried to pass off his emotion as pity for the insertion team because—well, first, they didn't know or understand the danger they were about to face, and second, they didn't have parachutes, so jumping from a disabled aircraft wasn't a possibility for them. Still, it was guilt the PJs felt, not pity. Saving themselves while others died was not their mission. No, PJs were sworn to the motto, "That Others May Live." So, Sergeant Sargent moved first, going back and sitting on the nylon sling seat mounted on the interior wall of the aircraft. He sat next to the commander of the insertion team, giving him a thumbs up to reassure him. But then he wished someone would reassure him. When he looked forward towards the cockpit, Jésus just turned and shrugged his shoulders, his dark silhouette outlined by the dim red light from the cockpit gauges.

After a moment, the second PJ moved to the sling seat across the cargo cabin from Sargent. He wasn't happy, but he fastened the seat belt. No, he wasn't happy at all. It was particularly difficult to be brave when only his partner knew what he was doing. But brave he was. He would occupy his time thinking just how long it would take him to undo his seat belt and sprint to the opening the ramp provided at the rear of the aircraft. He would also listen carefully for any sound out of the ordinary. Any sound, perhaps like one indicating metal on metal contact.

In the cockpit, Thibodeaux had called for the refueling checklist. They had run out the refueling probe and he was ready to take the aircraft into the pre-contact position where he would deftly combat the turbulence to put the probe in the refueling basket that was only barely visible. He flew in tandem with the larger aircraft by watching the dimly lit formation lights on the fuselage and wing of the C-130. It was a tricky bit of flying that challenged even the best of pilots, but Thibodeaux was very good at what he did.

Cleared to refuel, the aircraft began to buck as it entered the turbulence vortex of the prop wash. Thibodeaux flew the airplane with two fingers on the stick. The worst thing a pilot could do in this situation was over control his aircraft. He couldn't chase the basket or he would be there all night. He had to guess where the basket was going to be and fly his probe to that spot so that the probe and basket reached the spot simultaneously. Stretch watched the gauges with his right eye and the looming tail and fuselage of the C-130 with his left. His hands were clenched into balls, one resting on his kneeboard and the other on his right leg. Like the PJ, he mentally reviewed the bailout procedure for copilots. Still, in his heart he knew Thibodeaux would never leave the airplane while they had passengers on board, and in the back of his mind he knew he wouldn't either.

The airplane pitched and rolled as a narrow-beamed ship might in a heavy sea. Up, right, then left, then right, then down into the trough, then pitching nose up. Slowly they moved toward the basket.

In the cargo compartment, stomachs rolled and pitched with the motion of the aircraft. It was not the woman who retched, but the man who sat next to her.

But, after no more than sixty seconds, Thibodeaux drove the probe into the center of the refueling basket and was rewarded by a resounding click as the probe's over-center lock sealed inside the basket's one-way valve. Thibodeaux slid the aircraft up into the refueling position and looked down the vent tube at the end of the C-130's wing. Out of the turbulence, the aircraft flew smoothly as fuel flowed into the probe and then into the tanks of the oversized helicopter. Five hundred pounds of fuel, a thousand, and so on, until Thibodeaux had replaced all his expended fuel. At that point, he gently backed off the hose. As the probe disconnected there was a spray of atomizing fuel before the one-way valve could close.

"After refueling checklist," Thibodeaux ordered.

"King 33, Jolly 47." Thibodeaux growled on the radio. "Thanks for the gas, but next time you need to get the windows and check the tires. I thought you guys were a full service crew."

"Roger, Jolly. Copy windows and tires. Next time." There was relief in the C-130 pilot's voice.

Stretch's fists had, once again, become open hands.

Sargent relaxed the full body tension he had been holding through the entire refueling, and the second PJ silently thanked God.

Jésus just grinned. He had complete faith in his aircraft commander. Still, he unconsciously touched the crucifix he wore under his T-shirt.

The passengers were simply relieved that they were no longer being heaved to and fro in their seats. They had no understanding of what had just happened.

With the tanker out of sight, Thibodeaux commanded, "Navigation lights off."

"Lights off," Stretch replied as he flipped the switch to the off position.

Thibodeaux put the aircraft into a steep descent and headed for the navigation gate that would take him out of Thailand and into Laos. They had planned the refueling route so he would be headed north during the refueling. This brought him close to the border.

He and Stretch had worked out the route using overhead photography and tactical pilotage charts. The route was designed to take them through as many unoccupied valleys as possible so they could stay below any radar coverage. They also wanted to avoid villages and roads. Once through the starting gate Thibodeaux would fly according to heading, time, and airspeed. They would be in the treetops—not high enough to pick out landmarks as navigational aids. Since it was a moonless night, and even if they had been higher, it would be difficult to see much beyond the nose of the aircraft.

As they descended, Thibodeaux and Stretch went through the low level flight check list. They closed the Engine Air Particle Separators on the engines—"EAPS" as the checklist said. This would keep leaves and other debris from entering the engines. It would also cause the engines to run hotter. That was the tradeoff for not ingesting something that could cause a flameout or turbine stall. They turned on the low light level camera and infrared illuminator and confirmed their operation. They increased the throttles to 100 percent and turned down the level of the instrument panel's red lights. The kryptonite-green glow from the two TV monitors—one in front of each pilot—mixed with the red instrument lights to create an almost Christmas-like aura in the cockpit. Stretch noted that the green light from the monitors accentuated Thibodeaux's emerald-green eyes so that they seemed to glow. If Thibodeaux were not such a close friend, Stretch would have been afraid of the face he saw. His captain's eyes seemed those of a night-hunting predator.

Thibodeaux leveled the aircraft just above the trees and increased his speed to 140 knots. As they approached the Mekong River he commanded, "Stand by hack." Both he and Stretch reached up and reset their respective eight-day countdown clocks to zero. Then, at the northern side of the river, he reached up and pushed the start button on the clock's timer. Stretch did likewise as Thibodeaux commanded, "Hack."

Now it was a matter of staying in a black tunnel while maintaining a heading and airspeed. Stretch's job was to keep the camera pointed in front of the aircraft so they could see, in two dimensions, what lay ahead. But at 140 knots and with a very limited range on the camera, there would be almost no time to react should they encounter an unexpected obstacle.

In the back of the aircraft the PJs checked their newly arrived night vision goggles. The goggles were difficult to use because looking through them was like looking at two miniature television screens, each screen only an inch in front of each eyeball. In fact, it wasn't *like* that, it *was* that. Two small, flat TV screens almost pressed against your eyes. As with the larger monitors on the flight deck, there was no depth perception.

You had no idea how far something was from you, so you still had to feel your way.

The ride was bumpy since there was significant orographic turbulence from the drainage winds that flowed into the valleys from the mountains. Still, it was manageable. Thibodeaux tried to look outside as much as possible. It wasn't that he didn't trust the monitors, just that he felt better not looking at them. While he was happy to fly in all sorts of weather using his instruments with their red cockpit lights, the eerie green glow from the monitors combined with their inability to provide depth perception made him queasy. All the crew members were no doubt queasy, but he was responsible for the lives of eight people tonight and if he could minimize his own queasy sensations, he intended to do so. Still, looking outside there was only black. Even his much-better-than-average night vision wasn't sufficient to make out more than the next tree just to his right. It made him remember the tunnel he had traveled through while in the hospital, the blackness, and the occasional stop along the way to stare into the brown eyes of a nurse who reassured him and gave him another shot. Then it was back into the endless black tunnel winding through time and space.

It also made him think of his best friend in college ragging on him about flying at night. During college he had flown for a small commercial air firm and, on one occasion, had passed up an opportunity to go used car shopping with that friend because he'd wanted to fly up to Montgomery and back before dark. As he'd walked off, his friend had asked, "How are you gonna fly jets when you're afraid to fly at night?" Now here he was flying down India-ink black valleys with unseen hills climbing to his left and right as tree limbs slapped at his landing gear.

At nine minutes he prepared for his first turn. He climbed the aircraft fifty feet so that when he tilted his rotor it would not strike the trees on the down side of the turn. As the sweep second hand on the clock brought the minute hand to ten minutes elapsed, he began a timed turn to the left. Rolling out on the appropriate heading, he once again descended to just outside the grasp of the triple canopy forest below him.

In the back, the insertion team leader only knew they had turned. This was not his first insertion with this crew. In fact, it was his third insertion, and, he hoped, in ten days it would be his third covert extraction. Tran Duc Dan was only aware of the darkness. Even the small lights associated with various pieces of aircraft electrical equipment had been taped over with black electrician's tape so they would not glow. He appreciated the professionalism of the crew and the attention to detail they demonstrated. He wondered if the two agents seated across from him would demonstrate the same level of professionalism on their first mission into North Vietnam. "Well," he thought to himself, "I could cancel the mission if I had serious doubts about their commitment, but I'll take the calculated risk we all take in this profession."

Outside, the dark, moonless night wrapped the big helicopter in its protective folds as Thibodeaux made repeated turns, going from valley to valley until, after more than two hours, they arrived in the valley he sought.

He slowed the aircraft so that it barely moved above the treetops. The clearing he searched for was not large, so he would have to begin his landing approach as soon as he acquired it on the monitor.

He could not use the system as it had been designed. In the narrow confines of a mountain valley you could not fly the large patterns that the onboard computer needed for its approach-and-hover coupler mechanism that worked so well over water—where it had been designed and tested. Nor did the system's small stick, which protruded from the box to his right, give him the immediate control inputs he needed to avoid close-in obstacles. The system's fly-by-wire mechanism created only a split-second lag, but in the close quarters of these mountain valleys it didn't take more than a split-second to wander into a tree. No, he would use the cyclic and collective with which he always flew the aircraft. "Night Recovery" was a good enough system on paper, but in these jungles he depended on what he knew, and on that with which he was very good.

Suddenly they were on top of the southern edge of the clearing, and he began to drop the bird into the landing zone. With only the two dimensional view provided by the monitors, he had to feel his way. Even though he was practiced at this, every time was like the first time. Stretch operated the camera, keeping it pointed at the intended landing spot. The landing wasn't as soft as Thibodeaux normally managed because it was impossible to gauge distance to the ground during the last twenty feet— but it wasn't any rougher than an average copilot might make in daylight conditions.

"Team, this is the Captain." Thibodeaux intoned over the intercom. "You are cleared to exit the aircraft. *Chuc may man.*""Good luck" was one of the twenty or so Vietnamese phrases Thibodeaux had at his command.

Before handing his headset to Jésus, Tran replied, "Thank you, Captain, and may you successfully find your way home tonight." What he really meant was, "Please get home safe because if you don't I'm stuck in North Vietnam."

Sergeant Sargent and the number two PJ rolled the motorbikes off the ramp of the aircraft while Jésus escorted the two agents down the ramp and off to the right rear of the helicopter. Tran, even without night vision goggles, found his way down the ramp following Sergeant Sargent. The crew took the three team members and their motorbikes to the edge of the clearing and then headed back up the ramp. They were strapping themselves in as Thibodeaux, once again, ran the throttles up and lifted the big night bird into the moonless sky.

The helicopter's exit from North Vietnam would be just as exacting as its entry had been. The easy way out would have been to simply reverse the ingress route to go home. While it would have been easier, it would by no means have been safer. In fact, it would have been poor covert tradecraft to reverse the route. While the big helicopter could be made dark and difficult to see, it could not be made quiet. So anyone in the valleys through which it had flown entering the country would have heard the night bird. No, there would be a separate route home. As they left the edge of the clearing both pilots reset their clocks to zero.

The valleys on the way home seemed more turbulent. The aircraft bucked and yawed as the air cooled and flowed down the sides of the mountains creating crosswinds and pockets of vertical eddies, both up and down. The longer they watched the green screens and the more the turbulence tossed the aircraft from side to side, the further the pilots entered a two dimensional world. After they crossed the Mekong and landed briefly in a field to reinstall their star and bar placards and remove the tape covering the various pieces of electrical equipment, they remained in a two dimensional plane. But after they arose from the field and turned on their navigation lights and other regular aircraft lighting, they began to feel disoriented. The disorientation was even more pronounced with the green screens turned off. Now the cockpit was just red, and the shadows the red lights cast seemed to move in an otherworldly fashion. The fifty miles back to their base did not give them sufficient time to recover. In fact, they would not recover until sometime around mid-morning the following day. At least that had been their previous experience.

When the bright white of the landing lights lit the sky in front of them, both pilots felt not just light headed, but extremely nauseated as well. After landing they loaded their equipment into the flight line pickup and were motioned on board for the short ride to squadron headquarters. Thibodeaux, as was his usual practice, waved the truck on, declaring he needed to walk to regain his equilibrium. Stretch and the others rode in the back of the truck, and each bounce on the perforated steel planked flight line increased their nausea.

As usual, once the truck was out of sight, Thibodeaux stepped behind the nearest parked aircraft and, taking a small white bag from the leg pocket of his flight suit, barfed into it whatever food and liquid remained in his stomach. He barfed until all he could manage was bile. Sometimes he filled the bag, other times not so much, but once he stopped he found the nearest trash receptacle, disposed of the bag and walked to the squadron building after taking a swig of Listerine from the small plastic bottle he carried in a pocket of his survival vest. While he no longer felt the need to vomit, the nausea and vertigo would not leave him for a long while. Not even while he slept.

Although he felt better, he had discovered on earlier missions that the bright white fluorescent lights in the offices did not help dispel the effect of the vertigo; rather, they worsened it. So, he put on his sunglasses before entering the building. When he walked into the ready room he looked a little wan, but mostly he looked like a really cool pilot. The rest of the crew would, invariably, be in the washroom heaving their guts into toilets. Other squadron members who might be in the building at 0300 in the morning always thought Thibodeaux was somehow immune to the effects suffered by his crew. That was good for his reputation but, for the record, he always barfed first.

CHAPTER 5

FROM DARK TO LIGHT TO DARK

TRAN USED A SMALL FLASHLIGHT to find his team's way through the forest to the road he knew was two hundred meters west of the landing site. They pushed their small motorbikes, but once they reached the road they would start them up and ride towards the next village to the north. They would stop five kilometers outside the village so as not to enter during the middle of the night. Doing so would be suspicious, and suspicion was something spies always needed to avoid. They would find a place off the road and sleep late. Tran would once again go over their cover story with his agents and then they would enter the village sometime after noon.

Tran took the first watch as they bedded down for the rest of the night. As he sat staring into the darkness, he wondered if this would be the mission where something went wrong. "No," he said sotto voce, "not *if* something goes wrong. Something *always* goes wrong, but in the past I've always managed to walk or talk my way out of the situation. What I really mean is..." he asked himself, "...is this the time I won't be able to handle the situation?" He loved the dark, but he hated the waiting.

Danny Tran, as he was known to his college classmates at Yale, was one of the first Vietnamese graduates of that august institution. But he wasn't really Vietnamese. He had been born in Vietnam and had spent the first eleven years of his life there. He was fluent in the language and he certainly looked Vietnamese, but he didn't think of himself as Vietnamese.

His father and grandfather had been very successful businessmen in pre-World War II French Indochina, but after the war his father had understood that Ho Chi Minh would eventually come to power and had relocated the family from Hanoi to the United States. He had meant to go to France where he held citizenship, but an opportunity to become the director of raw rubber acquisition for a major American tire and rubber company had presented itself, and he had taken it.

So, eleven-year-old Tran Duc Dan moved with his family to Ohio where he had taken to the culture like he had been born into it. He became Danny Tran, a stalwart of his private school's wrestling and baseball teams. At Yale he became an All-Ivy wrestler as well as an honorable mention All-American second baseman. In college, during the ramp up of the Cold War, he had studied all things Russian, as well as political science in general. With his native Vietnamese and French, and a mastery of Russian gained during his four years at Yale, he had been a natural candidate when the CIA talent scouts at Yale began charting the progress of potential initiates for the recently formed clandestine agency. His first inkling of his recruitment had come during drinks and dinner at his Russian professor's home. At first he thought he might be a candidate for one of the secret societies like Skull and Bones. But, after a few meetings where he was progressively handed off from one person to another, it became clear the society that was interested in him was very secret, but much different than Skull and Bones. It was a secret society where, if your membership became known, you just might be on the short list to be assassinated or imprisoned and tortured. But he was Danny Tran, a true blue American from his flattop haircut to his Bass Weejun loafers. His country needed him.

And it had used him. With the appropriate forged Vietnamese or French documents, he could get close to Russian and East European diplomats and trade representatives. He wasn't looking so much to recruit one as to identify which of them were using their status to cover their real purpose of being themselves a spy or spymaster. It was the classic matchup of spy versus spy. Once identified, the Russian or Pole or Czech would be tracked and, when possible, false and misleading information would be passed their way. Danny would also attempt to identify their targets for recruitment, and, possibly, the agents they had already recruited and were meeting and directing. Then appropriate covert action measures would be taken in respect to those spies as well. It was the stuff of James Bond novels. No, actually, it was much better than James Bond novels. It was real life, and in the real life spy business, reputation, credibility, and even life itself were hazarded. The secret wasn't that this sort of thing occurred, the secret was in knowing who was involved and what, exactly, they were doing. Over the years his cover had held and, so far, he had not been identified as an American operative. Thus he remained in the field and had not moved to CIA Headquarters at Langley.

But now they needed him to try and confirm if, where, and how North Vietnam might be hiding US prisoners of war. It was thought all US POWs had been moved into a prison in downtown Hanoi after the failed Son Tay raid of 1970, but intelligence anomalies and bits and pieces of information reaching CIA Headquarters indicated there might still be individual POWs held outside Hanoi. Also, there was a possibility that Russians were involved in the activity and that some of the POWs might actually have been transferred to Russian control. Find out. This was his mission.

He wondered about the two neophyte agents in his charge. Sister and brother, they had extended family in some of the nearby villages. Their cover story was that they had been living in Hanoi but bombing had damaged their apartment building and they wanted to be safe. Children of a Vietnamese father and French mother, they had begun life in the middle class of business families in Hanoi but, with the ascendance of the Communist Party, the family had dropped further and further down the ladder of respectability as Communist Party members began to supplant the Indo-French members of Vietnamese society. The brother was educated, even having a year of university, but had become a cobbler because he wasn't a member of the Communist Party. The sister was an excellent tailor, and both carried the rudimentary tools of their trades in a large collapsible basket she held while riding sidesaddle on the pillion of his motorbike. They were good at keeping secrets. For many years they had managed a semi-successful existence in Hanoi.

Tran had found the two in a displaced persons camp in Laos. They had been captured crossing the border with badly forged documents that proclaimed they had family in South Vietnam which they were trying to reach. At least, they reasoned, they had made it out of North Vietnam—but now Tran had convinced them to return. Not because he had somehow persuaded them North Vietnam would lose the war, nor had he promised legal entry into South Vietnam. No, he held out the ultimate entitlement—access to the United States. It had taken a little to-ing and fro-ing with Langley, but he had persuaded the policy people that if answering the questions surrounding American POWs was both urgent and significant, then two more immigrants into the United States would be worth the cost. The agreement was that the two had to remain in North Vietnam for at least a year, travelling between rural areas, villages and cities to seek out information on POWs and Russians. That done, they would be resettled in the United States—unless, of course, some other mission could be identified where their particular skills and nationality would be of use. Tran, needless to say, did not share this other option with them. No sense in worrying any further ahead than tomorrow when they might at any moment encounter someone who could make their only future prison and death.

Tran's cover was that of a researcher for Russian interests in how much agricultural production could be increased by introducing tractors into the agricultural collectives. He possessed certain Russian and Vietnamese documents that would pass all but the most rigid of inspections in Hanoi or Moscow. Such documents allowed him to discuss the labor situation with farmers in what were very loosely run farm collectives. During his first two trips, he had learned that the collectives used more than 80 to 90 percent of what they produced for local needs. Only 10 to 20 percent of what they grew ended up headed for Hanoi or Haiphong. That certainly wasn't what the Communist Party intended.

His minions waited outside town while he circled around and entered the village from the north. In mid-afternoon, they entered from the east.

In that first village the man and the woman inquired about possible family members, but there was no one who remembered their father...perhaps in the next village. They remained two days before moving on. The man repaired some shoes and sandals, the woman did some mending of dresses and winter coats for members of the collective leaders' families. He asked if perhaps there were Europeans about who might need shoes or boots repaired. She asked if there were any foreign ladies who might need dresses sewn. No one remembered any foreigners having been in the village for years, unless of course, you counted the Communists from Hanoi who came to tell them they had become free, but that freedom meant they had to give part of their produce—give, mind you, not sell—to the people of Hanoi and Haiphong who protected them from the French and others who sought to exploit them. No one in the village remembered ever feeling threatened by the French; the French had not asked them to give their produce away, but rather had been anxious to buy some of it. It didn't make sense to the villagers that now they had to work other people's land, and that the land they had previously owned now belonged to the collective. No sense at all, but, no, they had not seen any foreigners, French or otherwise for years. Perhaps more to the east, over near some of the former French rubber plantations.

The man and the woman traded work for food, although they did have sufficient *đồng* in coins and a few bills to buy things if there was no work available. In the second village there was a rumor of foreigners who had been in a camp in the forest off the road to the north, but a quick ride out the road by Tran brought no success. On the eighth day, there was a road checkpoint they had to negotiate. They had learned of the checkpoint in the village before leaving, and Tran had instructed the brother and sister to go in front of him. When he came upon the checkpoint he was concerned when he saw their motorbike leaned against the guard hut. Yet when he stopped to show his papers to the guard he saw the couple inside the hut. The man was mending a pair of officer's boots and the woman was sewing up what appeared to be a tear in a shirt. He waited for them two kilometers down the road, just as earlier he had instructed them to do for him. After an hour, he worried. After two hours he worried more, but after three a dust cloud appeared up the road, and shortly thereafter they joined him. They were almost giddy with success. They had earned a few thousand đồng and learned much about Russians who had been in the area but were no longer there.

In the next village the young man asked one of the elders if perhaps there were people of quality in the area who might need leather work or sewing done. "People of quality, you ask," the elder replied. "We are farmers forced into groups with people with whom we would formerly have had no association. The only 'people of quality' now are those who are Party members. No, there are no people of quality hereabouts."

The reply did not surprise the cobbler but he was careful not to express sympathy for the elder's comments because in Hanoi he had learned the Communist Party had spies everywhere, and to speak against the Party could earn you a prison sentence. It was this culture he and his sister had tried to escape.

On the ninth day, Tran showed the couple the site where he would reappear on his next visit. That visit would not be for several weeks since the couple could now serve as the eyes and ears that he, himself, had been on previous missions. When he left, they were to keep traveling through the region seeking information about potential POW sites and Russian presence. If they discovered any factual knowledge about the presence of POWs, they were to use the communication device he left with them.

Concealed in the small, hand-operated sewing machine the girl carried in the basket was a simple burst transmitter. By stringing out a spool of wire thread for an antenna, they could send a series of bursts on a single frequency. Three bursts meant, "need to meet." Four bursts meant, "have definite information on POWs." Five bursts meant, "trouble." They had memorized where and when Tran would appear if they sent him a signal.

On the tenth day Tran hugged both of them, buoyed their spirits by reminding them of their future in the United States, and then rode off towards the site where the black bird would meet him at midnight.

At midnight-plus-two Sergeant Sargent rolled Tran's motorbike up the ramp while Tran strapped himself into the sling seat. At midnight-plus-four the black bird lifted into the tops of the trees.

Tran spent the entire return flight reviewing all he had done, the little he had gained, and the prodigious perils he and his agents had faced. By the time the crew dropped him off at his secret rendezvous site in Thailand, he was no longer Tran the spymaster, but Danny Tran, American through and through, and willing to hazard all dangers in order to return safely those who had been captured. How appropriate, he thought, that his missions were being flown by Air Rescue pilots whose motto was "That Others May Live."

CHAPTER 6

SOMETIMES IT'S GOD
YOU STRUGGLE WITH

WHEN THE REMNANTS OF A typhoon roared up the Mekong during monsoon season, you were going to get wet. The regular rains were bad enough, but when the monsoon system arrived, the only possible option was to find a place to hunker down and wait. Thus Captain Thibodeaux, Air Rescue pilot extraordinaire, raconteur, and general all-round good guy—well, at least half the squadron thought so, mostly the enlisted guys—waited. Ricocheting from side to side as he made his way down the hall, he skipped to avoid the catch pots whose water was being periodically emptied out the doors—only to later find its way back into the building through the plywood floor which geysered fountains up through its cracks when stepped upon. Water leaked from the ceiling, too, having been driven into the overhead by the fifty-plus-mile-an-hour winds. The window screens, never meant to stop anything smaller than a housefly, redirected the horizontal rain only enough for it to run, as if from an open faucet, down the sills and onto the floor.

"Squadron commander wants to see you, sir," said Master Sergeant Meadows, the new administrative noncommissioned officer in charge, as Thibodeaux passed the administration office.

"Roger that," Thibodeaux replied, almost kicking a two-gallon coffee tin brimming with water.

He made his way to the end of the building and entered flight operations to check the weather writer that was hooked up to the weather shop. It still showed a 125-foot ceiling with winds blowing out of the east at thirty—gusting to forty-five—knots, which, to the non-flyers, was about fifty miles an hour or so. Thibodeaux, being from the Gulf Coast, was at home in hurricanes and tropical storms, so he wasn't as concerned as some of his squadron mates. He did worry about his aircraft, but—knowing that he had personally supervised the tie down and sandbagging of the gear—he was satisfied there was little to do but wait out the storm and then pick up the pieces.

While checking the writer, he noticed a group gathered around the squadron's UHF/VHF/HF radio set. The group was just dispersing when the teletype began to hum and type out an incoming message. The teletype was on a dedicated line between the squadron, the squadron's headquarters at Third Rescue Group, and their ultimate commanders at Seventh Air Force at Tan San Nhut Air Base in Vietnam. Third Rescue used the line to transmit operational plans and orders to the squadron at Nakhon Phanom. The squadron's commander, who had been part of the group gathered round the radio, stepped over to the teletype and began lifting up the long sheet of paper as it was pushed out by the rollers. Reading it as it rolled up, he waited for the last few clicks of the typewriter's keys ending the message before tearing it off the machine. His face expressed no emotion as he turned, message in hand, to face Thibodeaux and said,

"You would think someone at Third would have stopped this silly thing. I mean, when you think about it, no one at Third is NRS qualified, but at least they should know better than to try to fly a helicopter in these conditions."

Apparently they didn't. Thibodeaux read the telex, then pursed his lips and raised an eyebrow as he handed it back:

From: Commanding General, 7th Air Force
Via: Commanding Officer, 3rd Air Rescue Group
To: Commanding Officer, 40th Air Rescue Squadron
Subject: Evacuation of Wounded at Mukdahan

URGENT

Upon receipt this order 40th Rescue will launch a second attempt to evacuate eight wounded Air Force and Army personnel along with flight surgeon and anyone else he designates as necessary from Mukdahan, Thailand. Collective wisdom here indicates darkness should prove no impediment since 40th is equipped with Night Recovery System aircraft.

Effort should also be made to transport necessary repair equipment to recover Jolly 53 which aborted upon landing Mukdahan 1830Z today.

Respond soonest with tail number, call sign, number of passengers and crew of NRS Rescue aircraft dispatched.

Signed: Hadley M. Johnson, Maj Gen, Chief of Air Operations

"I wonder if they think the Night Recovery System negates rain and wind as well as darkness?" The squadron commander was beginning to wind himself up. "Don't they know we haven't even been able to make the 'night' part of the damn system work as advertised? We've had the goddamn things out here almost a year, and we still haven't made a rescue at night using the system." His face began to twitch ever so slightly, the left side of his mouth curling into what would quickly become a sneer unless checked.

Thibodeaux, knowing resistance to Seventh Air Force orders was futile, and also knowing the commanding officer didn't need to explode in front of so many subordinates, quickly interceded with a question to the duty officer.

"Do we have an NRS crew in crew rest?"

"All the NRS crews are in the building, and I guess they all have the same amount of crew rest or other duty limitations," replied the captain at the counter.

"So, that makes it easy." Casting a quick look at the squadron commander who shrugged his shoulders, Thibodeaux instructed, "Have crew zero seven report to the ready room for briefing, and have the chief of maintenance alert the mechanics he needs to send down to retrieve Jolly 53. Have them load whatever equipment is necessary into the back of Jolly 47. Alert the crew chief to prepare 47 for launch. Full fuel load. Call air tactical control and have them man the tower. See if you can raise 53 on the HF radio at the hospital in Mukdahan and tell them we'll need some kind of landing zone light when we get down there."

"*If* they get down there," one sergeant in the corner of the room whispered to another. "No way I want to be on that aircraft!" Being an administrative clerk, there was actually no way he would be on the aircraft—so his concern was, at best, an expression of sympathy with the enlisted crew members and mechanics who would have to be aboard Jolly Green 47.

The other NRS pilots and crew members in the room felt a great relief sweep over them, tempered by just the slightest twinge of jealousy, as they wondered, "Why does Thibodeaux's crew get all the glory missions?" Still, it was a glory mission only if successfully completed, and success in this undertaking was a matter of considerable doubt.

Thibodeaux gathered his crew in the briefing room only long enough to give the basics of the mission, noting this was not a rescue attempt per se, but an evacuation mission. He expected no hostile action, given the weather, and although those being evacuated had been wounded by a land mine explosion, there was no indication of hostiles in the immediate area. While the crew would prepare as if they were going into a hostile situation, they would not have their number three gun since it would be removed to allow the on-load and off-load of rolling maintenance equipment needed for the repair of Jolly 53.

The pre-flight was a nightmare as Jésus and Stretch checked items on the aircraft. Along with Thibodeux, they wore ponchos over their flight suits—which did little to keep them dry as they climbed over and underneath the aircraft. When Thibodeaux duck-crawled under the aircraft to inspect the Doppler radar dome, he found it filled with water that would deny him the use of the Doppler set. Since it seldom worked correctly, even in the dry season, he wasn't overly concerned.

Jésus gathered the nine mechanics who would be riding along as passengers, making sure he briefed them on airsickness bags. He asked the aircraft crew chief to go back to the hangar and get extra bags because he knew that there would be more than a little turbulence on this flight—and also that maintenance types were notoriously bad flyers.

Then they pushed the 2,500-pound hydraulic mule—which would be used to test Jolly 53's hydraulic system—onto the aircraft and secured it with cargo tie-down straps. Jésus insisted on several extra straps because the last thing they needed was for this piece of machinery to start moving around the aircraft during flight. Jésus insisted on the same additional security for the wooden crates that held replacement hydraulic dampers and fittings for the repair.

Thoroughly wet, Thibodeaux and Stretch climbed into their seats, already squishing water as they sat down. The rain had found its way inside the aircraft, and both the nylon cushions were soaked. It was going to be a very unpleasant night.

The start-up and pre-taxi checklists went quickly. When Thibodeaux contacted the tower for taxi instructions he thought he could hear snickering in the background as the controller gave him clearance. Because of the weight, passengers, and weather, Thibodeaux elected to make a rolling takeoff. He would taxi to the end of the runway and turn around on the numbers. As he taxied across the perforated steel planking that was the Jolly parking area, the weight of the aircraft squeezed water up through the perforations, creating large geysers which, caught between the wind and the helicopter's downwash, swirled into airborne eddies that made visibility even worse than it had been. At least the marshalers were using lighted wands and the wing-walkers were keeping him clear of other parked aircraft. He taxied slowly toward the runway.

Not having a system to speak directly with the passengers since there weren't enough headsets, Thibodeaux asked Jésus and the PJs to make sure everyone's seat belt was tight and that everyone had an available airsickness bag. When he received assurances such was the case, he asked Stretch for 105 percent power. When the gauges indicated his turbines were at that level, he pulled up on the collective, pushed forward on the stick, and they were rolling. Even on the runway the wind tried to move the heavy aircraft sideways, but Thibodeaux held the tip path plane—the path described by the rotating helicopter blade tips—into the quartering wind, and about a hundred feet down the runway the Jolly lifted into the air. Almost immediately she skewed her nose to the right as she streamlined into the wind. Thibodeaux adjusted his angle on the nose so they were climbing in a crab.

Twenty feet up, the aircraft stuttered and almost stopped as the first wind shear hit. At fifty feet, a gust from the side moved the helicopter off the centerline of the runway. Thibodeaux fought the controls, regaining his heading after each shock. Already it was clear he was going to have to muscle his way through the entire mission. At two hundred feet, they hit the second shear.

"Jesus Christ!" It was Stretch, yelling as the bottom fell out of their lift and his stomach. In the rear of the aircraft, faces turned white, then green, as dinners neared the tops of esophagi. Surely the next major jolt would overcome them. Bags at the ready, the passengers swayed from side to side as the gusts swung the tail this way and that.

Thibodeaux held onto the controls tightly. His stomach was not affected because he was too busy wrestling the airplane back to heading and altitude. He felt badly for Stretch. "Grab the controls with me and hold on," he grunted to Stretch, who thankfully reached out to anchor himself with his own cyclic and collective. For Thibodeaux, Stretch's grip only added pressure when he made corrections, but for Stretch, contact with the controls allowed him to concentrate on something other than keeping his bologna sandwich down.

Helicopters shake all the time, but good pilots learn to differentiate between the "always there" rattles and shakes, and the unusual ones that indicate problems. That differentiation was almost impossible on this flight. Thibodeaux could not place any of the noises he heard above the roar of the wind. One noise was an arrhythmic ringing. It was almost like a number of bells being rung without pattern. He kept trying to place the sound in his head but could not.

He had hoped the winds would stabilize as he got higher off the ground. High winds made heavy orographic turbulence at low altitudes because of hills and forests, but at a higher level, the flight might be smoother. Yet the higher Thibodeaux climbed, the less he liked what was happening. He was sure his ground speed was dropping almost precipitously.

When he spoke to Joker, the Rescue command post, Thibodeaux's voice sounded exceedingly choppy because of the wild bull of an aircraft he was riding. "Joker, Jolly 47. Can the weather guys estimate the winds aloft? Say, four to nine thousand feet? I think I'm having a hard time making headway."

"Roger, Jolly. Weathermen estimate winds at four to ten thousand feet at between sixty and one hundred knots, probably blowing from the south-southeast. Does that help?"

"Roger. Understand sixty-to-one-hundred-knot possible head wind. Jolly will be flying below four thousand feet."

At Joker, the squadron commander turned to the group following him about. "Going to make for one helluva rough flight. He'll only have intermittent radio and TACAN—Tactical Air Navigation System—contact once he gets south of here." He settled in at a desk, his feet on its corner.

Within twenty minutes, the cargo compartment of Jolly Green 47 smelled like a fraternity house the morning after a toga party. Full airsickness bags lined the bulkhead under the nylon sling seats. Empty bags were being held at the ready under each passenger's chin. Even the PJs were losing their lunches. The smell had made its way to the flight deck, and Stretch was beginning to think seriously about whether he really needed that bologna sandwich or not.

The rain continued to hit the windscreen so hard it was impossible to see out, but even absent the rain there would have been nothing but blackness. At night, Thailand offered little in the way of lights on the ground with which a pilot could orient himself or gauge his progression. Thibodeaux had lost his TACAN fix and was navigating by dead reckoning—which in this case meant he was pretty much guessing.

Thibodeaux could still hear the bells ringing, sometimes rhythmically, sometimes as if they were alarm bells. "Jésus, can you hear that noise that sounds like bells? If you can, will you try and identify the area it's coming from?"

Not able to unstrap himself and move around, Jésus fixed his eyes on a given space and waited until he could hear the sound. Finding nothing in that space he would move his eyes to another and wait. After about five minutes he identified the sound as a chain on the towing bar of the hydraulic mule. He liked having something to do because while he was concentrating on finding the sound he had not needed to retch into his bag.

More than an hour after losing TACAN, Thibodeaux believed he had the aircraft somewhere near his objective. He tried to raise Jolly 53 on the HF set.

"Jolly 53, Jolly 47. Over."

"Jolly 53, Jolly 47. Over."

On his third attempt he heard, "Jolly 47, Jolly 53. Go."

"Jolly 53, best estimate is we are in the vicinity. Can you hear our rotors?" At fifty thousand pounds and with five thirty-foot rotor blades, Jolly Greens made lots of noise.

Then, off to Thibodeaux's left, the sky began to light up. It looked as if he had entered Times Square in a dense fog. Yellows and reds diffused throughout the clouds like neon signs selling Coke or Pepsi. It took a moment, but Thibodeaux realized exactly where he was. He banked the aircraft to the right.

"Stretch, our friends, the Phatet Lao, have helped us out. We're over Savannah Ket. Those fireworks are the gunners welcoming us to Laos."

And then he heard, "Jolly 47, we can hear your rotors. You sound east of us."

"Roger that, 53. We're approaching from the east. How are your conditions? Over."

"Jolly 47, we're in a soccer field in the center of the village. Terrain is hills to the west, a five-hundred-foot radio mast to the south. Field is flooded. DO NOT, repeat, DO NOT, make approach to touchdown or your gear will sink in the mud. Jolly 53 is in the center of the field so you'll have to land in one of the corners. The field is lit by the headlights of three pickups. Rain is heavy but we estimate the ceiling at one to two hundred feet. Winds are mostly from the south and strong. Recommend approach from north or east."

Thibodeaux quickly assessed his situation. An approach from the east was out because even if the Phatet Lao were firing blindly, they might get lucky and hit his aircraft with one of their anti-aircraft guns or some small arms fire, especially if he was low and at approach speed. An approach from the south or west was out of the question because of the terrain and radio tower. That left him with the approach from the north, but if he had to go around he would have to break to the east, taking him right back over the Laotian guns. He had not been able to raise the frequency of the radio transmitter the mast served, so it must be off the air. That was too bad, since otherwise he could have shot an ADF—Automatic Direction Finder—approach using the mast as his reference point. Still, that might be his best answer. An ADF-like approach.

"Jolly 53, vector us in by sound and tell me when I'm directly overhead." Thibodeaux dropped to one thousand feet above the ground as indicated by his radar altimeter.

"Roger 47. You're getting louder but sound south of us. Turn north." Thibodeaux turned more to the right. "More north." Thibodeaux continued his turn. "You're getting closer. More west." Thibodeaux stopped his turn. "Sounds like you're heading right for us. Countdown, five, four, three, two, one. You're overhead."

As 53 said "overhead" Thibodeaux rolled his airplane to an almost due north heading and then turned back westward thirty degrees to create an offset from the original heading. As he did so he punched the timer on his eight-day clock. The airplane bucked in the turbulence but he held her steady. After one minute, he rolled into a thirty-degree bank to the right, and set up a five-hundred-feet-per-minute rate of descent. He held the turn for thirty seconds, rolling out on the reciprocal of the northerly heading he had initially turned to over Mukdahan. He kept his descent going. The airplane shook, rattled, rolled, and yawed as the winds buffeted it.

The passengers were all but exhausted, their strength ebbing after having gripped the aluminum tubes that constituted their seats and the aircraft bulkhead supports for almost two hours. Stretch leaned forward, peering out a windscreen into the Stygian darkness in front. Thibodeaux kept his eyes on his flight instruments. From the corner of his left eye he was constantly aware of the radar altimeter. He was getting close to the ground. He was already below a non-precision approach decision altitude. As he got lower, he slowed the aircraft. He was below normal approach airspeed.

"Lights, one o'clock!" Stretch sighed loudly. Thibodeaux banked to the right.

Sure enough, Jolly 53 was sitting in the middle of the field and the corners weren't all that big. There was actually little light since the headlights on the trucks were so low. The field was almost completely in shadows created by the hulking presence of Jolly 53. Still, Thibodeaux could see well enough to discern a place to put 47. As he hovered his still heavy bird over the spot, his ninety-mile-an-hour downwash created a hurricane-like swirling of water and mud. He took the airplane down as close as he could get. As he did, Jésus jumped out the door, two flashlight wands in hand, and made his way to the front of the aircraft. Standing well beyond the rotors, he marshaled Thibodeaux into a lower hover. The aircraft wheels descended just into the top of the water. Then, ever so slowly, Jésus brought the pilot down even further—until the bottom of the aircraft's wheels were deep in the water, but not touching the mud. He held his arms horizontal in a "hold your hover" motion and then ran back to the door and climbed aboard. He plugged into the interphone system again.

"Captain, you're about six inches above the mud. Hold her there. I'm going to get the mule off the back, but you'll have to move forward as we do it since the mule won't roll in the mud once its wheels are off the back. Watch my signals." He then gave instructions to the mechanics and the two PJs.

One PJ stood to the right rear of the aircraft and relayed arm signals to Jésus who had taken the wands and was again in front of 47. As the mechanics pushed the mule to the rear, Thibodeaux could feel the helicopter's center of gravity shifting, and he ever so gently made corrections in his hover. As the mule began to drop from the back he felt the aircraft's tail dragging and its nose rising. Jésus was motioning him forward. With almost imperceptible movements, Thibodeaux raised the collective and pushed forward on the cyclic. As the aircraft moved forward the mule plopped off the back as if a standing cow had just delivered a calf. The nose now went down and the tail up. Thibodeaux caught it quickly, just keeping the nose gear from plowing into the mud. Stopping the porpoise, he recovered to his six-inch hover and remained there. Maintaining position while boxes and personnel were moving in the aircraft was less of a challenge than stabilizing the helicopter while the mule was being off-loaded, but he was still hypervigilant to movement as he hovered, his wheels just in the water.

Moving the equipment and personnel had taken about half an hour, although to Thibodeaux it seemed a longer time than he had spent in college. The visual references for his hover kept disappearing as the wind and rain whipped up eddies that hit his rotor downwash. If not for Jésus standing in front of him, wands in hand, he would have had almost no reference. The lights from the trucks continued to cast long, low shadows that came and went with the intensity of the rain.

One of the PJs said:

"Sir, we can't get the survivors up near the landing zone in vehicles because of the road conditions, so we're going to have to carry each one on a stretcher for about a quarter mile. Since the mechanics are still throwing up and we need some people to hold ponchos over the injured, we'll have to use some locals. Between us and Jolly 53's PJs, it's going to take a while."

"Roger, understand," was all Thibodeaux could say. Anything else would only have slowed the process. He did think about taking off and trying to find his way in again, but quickly dismissed that idea. He had to continue to hover his aircraft at six inches. He had held long hovers before at one hundred or two hundred feet. He had hovered with water blowing around him when practicing sea recoveries, but those hovers had lasted fifteen or twenty minutes at most. He had already been holding Jolly 47 up for over thirty minutes, and now he was beginning to experience the cramping that came with constant muscle exertion in one position. The last time he had felt this cramped was when they had shoved him into that too-small box with a hood over his head as he was being trained to resist interrogation if captured.

At that moment, a new voice came over the interphone. "How you doing, Jean-Louis?"

Stretch turned to his right as a new head appeared in the flight deck pass-through. It was Foster Leeman, the chief of standardization and the senior of the two pilots on Jolly 53.

"Doing just fine, Foster," Thibodeaux replied.

"Listen, Jean-Louis. Dana and I were talking. We think you guys did a great job getting down here, but you're probably airsick. I saw the green faces and bags that came out of the back of your aircraft, and the mechanics are still throwing up in the guest house. I know you have to be tired. We've been down here all day, so we're rested, and we're thinking we'll take your aircraft and you can get some rest while the mechanics work on 53. I'll have Dana slide in for Stretch, and you'll give him the airplane, and then I'll replace you."

From between gritted teeth Thibodeaux answered, "Damned nice of you guys to offer, but Stretch and I are just fine. Right, Stretch?"

Stretch, using his most eloquent Air Force Academy language, replied, "Damn straight, Bubba."

"Yeah, but since we're standardization pilots and this is a mission with critically injured personnel we, ah....want to have the most, ah....experienced pilots on board." Leeman really wanted the airplane.

Stretch was about to ask him if he had a nomination for a Silver Star like Thibodeaux, but before he could form his question, Thibodeaux cut in. "Listen Foster, I know you'd like to get a save or two. God knows, it's tough for you guys that have all this flying time but no saves yet. I'd really like to help you and Dana, but Seventh specifically directed an NRS crew take this mission and I'm not going to fight Seventh Air Force. So as much as I'd like to help you, we're under orders. Now, I think this might go faster if you and Dana would help carry those litters."

Leeman backed out of the space and took off the headset.

As he left, Stretch asked, "What were you going to do if he kept pushing? Him being chief of evaluation and all?

"Oh, I don't know," Thibodeaux ruminated, his head never turning, his eyes never leaving his hover mark. "Probably pull rank or something. I'm senior to him on the service list. He'd have had to find some reason to declare me unqualified to fly, and he isn't going to go that far. Besides, these guys are way out of crew rest. They launched well before noon and it's midnight now. They've been in duty status the entire day, so they would be violating MAC manual 60-1."

Nothing more passed between the two except Stretch verbally counting the injured as they were loaded aboard. Thibodeaux continued to feel the muscles in his back, neck, arms, and legs tighten into rock-like solidity. Poor Jésus still stood in front of the aircraft providing a hover reference, his arms flagging every so often. He struggled to maintain his upright and locked position against 47's rotor wash as well as against the wind gusts, which arrived unannounced.

Thibodeaux, glancing at his fuel gauges, noted, "Bangkok's out of the solution now. Raise NKP on HF and tell them we'll be recovering there."

Stretch did as requested, and NKP told them a C-130 with litters and medical personnel was on standby. Field conditions were now ceiling at one hundred feet with a half-mile visibility, and winds out of the south at twenty-five, gusting to thirty-five. At least conditions at NKP were improving, but Jolly 47 was still 150 miles south, hovering in water up to her wheel hubs.

At 0020 local time, the PJ announced all the injured were on board and the flight surgeon wanted to talk to the pilot. He put a headset on the doctor's head. Leaning forward into the flight deck area, the doctor put out his hand, as if to shake hands with Thibodeaux.

Reaching over and grabbing the hand, Stretch said over the interphone:

"He's a little busy at the moment, Doc. He's flying the airplane. What can we do for you?"

"Oh..." the doctor replied, not really understanding that Thibodeaux was actually holding the aircraft off the ground. "Ah...we have two serious shrapnel head wounds back here and I'm concerned that if we go much above a thousand feet they may hemorrhage."

"So Doc, not above a thousand feet. Roger that," Thibodeaux noted. Turning his head ever so slightly towards Stretch, he said, "Hit Jésus with your flashlight and let's get out of here."

Stretch used the button on his flashlight to signal Jésus who dropped his arms and came at a run—or at least an attempted run—through the foot-or-more of water. He climbed into the aircraft through the crew door. Plugging his helmet back into the intercom he checked that everyone was strapped into the sling seats and that the stretchers were secured along the walls of the airplane. Then he said, "Cleared for forward flight."

Thibodeaux picked 47 up to what he thought was about a fifteen-foot hover, "Clear tail right."

"Clear right," a PJ responded.

Thibodeaux pedal-turned the aircraft until he was on the northerly heading he wanted, and then, pushing the nose over slightly, he pulled collective. Taking off downwind was always an experience, and in this case, the tail of the aircraft lifted as the wind gusts struck it. But after the turbulence they'd encountered on the way down, this push seemed more like a gentle shove for good luck than an attempt to overturn the aircraft.

Climbing through five hundred feet on the radar altimeter, Thibodeaux said, "Copilot's airplane. Level at one thousand feet above ground level."

Stretch put his hands on the controls, "I've got it. Understand level at one thousand feet."

Thibodeaux relaxed, trying to flex his arms and legs. The pain in his back would remain because he could not leave his seat to stretch. He used this opportunity to check his gauges, computing in his head how much fuel he would have when he reached NKP. "Well…" he said to Stretch, "We aren't going to be able to climb up into those sixty-mile-an-hour tail winds we fought on the way down, and we won't be able to pick up the TACAN until we're almost on top of the base, but I think we'll be alright."

While Stretch flew the aircraft, Thibodeaux raised NKP to give them an update. The HF connection was a little shaky given the storm conditions, but with a few repeats they communicated what they needed to. Thibodeaux gave them an estimated time of arrival at NKP, noting the seriousness of the injured. They understood.

After Stretch had fought the turbulence for three-quarters of an hour, Thibodeaux took the airplane back in hand. He thought he knew where he was, but wished he could have some type of reassurance. Then he realized the strobes showing on his radar homing and warning system weren't all radar-controlled guns out of Laos to his east. One was from the north. With a tremendous sense of relief, he realized it had to be Invert, the NKP radar controller.

"Invert. Invert. Jolly Green 47."

"Jolly Green 47. Invert. Iden?"

Stretch hit the toggle on the IFF— Identification Friend or Foe—control head.

"Jolly Green 47, Invert. Radar contact thirty-five miles south of channel eighty-seven. Please state intentions."

Thibodeaux and Stretch looked at each other and smiled— expressions that appeared weirdly in the subdued red light of the Jolly's cockpit.

"Invert, Jolly 47 requesting radar vectors to GCA—ground control approach—channel eighty-seven."

"Roger. Jolly 47. Altimeter twenty-seven point eighty-eight. Descend to five thousand feet and turn right heading zero one zero."

"Understand altimeter twenty-seven point eighty-eight, turning to zero one zero. Invert, be advised Jolly 47 is at one thousand feet and can go no higher."

"Roger 47. Understand one thousand feet. That explains why we couldn't find you sooner. You were too low."

"Piece of cake," Stretch almost sighed.

But then the red lights began to flicker on and off. "Shit!" was the tall one's next comment. "I think we've got water in the DC electrical bus." Just as he finished, the cockpit dropped into total darkness except for the caution panel—and the master caution—lights which had illuminated to tell the pilots they had lost instrument lighting.

As if he had planned for this, Jésus, who was standing in the cargo compartment leaning into the flight deck, calmly took a penlight out of his pocket and pointed its beam at the attitude indicator. He reached up and took the penlight out of Thibodeaux's left-sleeve pen-holder and trained its beam on the horizontal situation indicator. Feet braced against the gun box below the flight deck, he struggled to maintain his balance as Jolly 47 bounced in the turbulence.

Stretch, following Jésus' lead, had taken out his own penlight and was shining it on the altimeter.

"Jolly 47, turn left heading three five three. Currently thirty miles south of channel eighty-seven."

Thibodeaux gently banked the aircraft.

"Jolly 47, NKP. How do you read? Over."

"Jolly 47 has you loud and clear."

"Jolly 47, this is your final controller. Stand by GCA into NKP. Altimeter two seven point eight eight, winds one eight zero variable one five zero at twenty-five, gust thirty-five. Conditions at NKP—one-hundred-foot ceiling, half-mile visibility. RCR—runway condition report—of twelve. Do you desire an expedited downwind approach?"

"Jolly 47. Two seven point eight eight. That is affirmative, GCA. We'd like to get on the ground as soon as possible."

And, true to Stretch's earlier assessment, the rest really was a piece of cake—although given the lack of instrument lights, Thibodeaux and his crew would have preferred the cake to have been a birthday cake for an octogenarian…with 80 candles lighting up the cockpit!

After acquiring the runway at one hundred feet, Thibodeaux thanked the ground controllers and made a visual approach, turning into the wind for a hovering touch down. A "follow me" truck led him to a parking spot where he was tail-to-tail with the C-130.

Once the wounded had been transferred to the big aircraft, Thibodeaux was instructed to taxi the Jolly to another parking spot so the propeller wash of the C-130 wouldn't blow him over as the C-130 pilot pushed up power to taxi out.

As he was shutting down his aircraft, Thibodeaux could see the landing lights and the rotating beacons of the C-130 reflecting off the rooster tail of water it created as it roared down the runway, lifting quickly into the still-black sky from which rain would continue to fall for the next two days.

Thibodeaux recommended his crew, and all the mechanics that had survived the trip down, for an Air Medal—not just because of the weather, but because they were all volunteers and 47 had been shot at over Savannah Ket. Seventh Air Force disapproved the request with the comment that medals were not awarded for "doing your job."

In later years, deep into his life, if—after three or so Sazerac cocktails—you could convince Thibodeaux to speak of his adventures in Indochina, he would tell you this story and claim it was the best piece of flying he ever did.

CHAPTER 7

DAMNED FEW LEFT

IT HAD NOT RAINED WITH any gusto for the past two days, but Thailand, Laos, and Cambodia still looked like one giant rice paddy. Everything was wet. The hoped-for end to the monsoon season might be near, but the humidity, as always, was at the upper end of the hygrometer. Thibodeaux's helmet lining was wet and chaffed his forehead. The seat cushion was wet, his flight suit was wet, his underwear was wet, his hair was wet. Hell, he was just wet—and everything around him was wet. His socks rubbed, the waistband on his boxers cut, his T-shirt stuck to his back. He would have been miserable if he hadn't been so angry.

The pages of the AF 781 aircraft log stuck together as he tried to enter the details of the flight and record that the aircraft needed to be inspected for an intermittent vibration when the landing gear was raised or lowered. He suspected the utility hydraulic system needed to be bled—that it probably had air in the lines causing momentary hiccups. He had gotten much the same vibration when he lowered the ramp just before landing.

Stretch came out of the aircraft's crew door, classified brief-case in hand. Inside the briefcase he had the Jefferson encryption wheel and the daily codes they would have used if it had been necessary to transmit or receive something in code. Thibodeaux hoped they would soon receive the KY-28s they had been prom-ised. Automatically encrypted radios would certainly make things a lot easier. For one thing, they wouldn't have to lug that damned briefcase around everywhere they went.

The stuck-together pages just heightened his frustration. He almost tore them apart. Stretch offered to take over the job, but instead of handing him the book Thibodeaux pressed on, trying to get the next page of the 781 to unstick from the page he had just finished.

He reached down and took the switchblade out of the leg pocket on his flight suit, flicked the blade out, and used the super sharp point to separate the pages. Why hadn't he thought of this earlier? As he got the page flipped, the squad-ron commander's pickup skidded to a stop on the perforated steel planking in front of the HH-53 and a furious lieutenant colonel emerged.

Stretch turned to Jésus, "Uh-oh. This ought to be a humdinger."

"You think?" was the only reply Jésus could come up with.

The door to the truck was left open.

"What *on earth* did you say to the general?!" Schaffer's voice started an octave above its normal pitch.

"Told him to stay the fuck off the radios."

"What??"

"I told him to stay the fuck off the radio while I was making a rescue. Simple as that. I'm in the middle of a rescue and this one-star son of a bitch is ordering me to leave the area. Who the hell does he think he is?"

"But you did it on Guard channel, where the entire world could hear! I mean, your transmission overrode every other transmission in Southeast Asia! Even the Strategic Air Command heard it!"

Thibodeaux, looking just as furious as the colonel, shoved his pen back in the sleeve pocket of his flight suit, slammed shut the cover of the AF 781—well, slammed as much as he could slam the flexible piece of plastic holding the seriously damp pieces of paper—and handed the log book to Jésus,

"When somebody's shooting at you, you don't key the mike and ask some son of a bitch to come up on a secure channel so you can tell him to fuck off. You just do it. He was on Guard channel. I was on Guard channel."

"Well, he's charging you with failure to obey a direct order."

"Doesn't hold water, does it?"

"What do you mean, doesn't hold water?"

"Well, an order has to be legal before it becomes possible to disobey it, right?"

"Yeah, so what? The guy's a brigadier. You're a captain."

"Yes, but he's a Seventh Air Force brigadier and I'm a Rescue captain, and when there's a rescue underway who runs the fucking air war? Not Seventh Air Force. We do. Rescue. *Res ipsa loquitur.* It speaks for itself. Any decent JAG will argue jurisdiction. The brigadier didn't have any. I was the on-scene commander, and the decision to remain was mine and mine alone. Just being the Blue Chip—Seventh Air Force—controller doesn't give him authority to intervene in a rescue operation. That orbiting command post doesn't have any authority when there's a rescue underway."

Schaffer drew the flat of his hand slowly from his forehead down to his chin, in the process scraping a pint or more of sweat and condensation from his face. "Well, you didn't have to tell him to stay the fuck off the radio. Seventh is screaming for your scalp."

"Well, as far as I'm concerned they can have it."

"For Pete's sake, don't say that Jean-Louis. You've got a great career going. You're a shoo-in for promotion to major and a command slot, if—that is—we can get you out of this. What happened?"

"Listen Boss, can't we go in, let me get debriefed and you listen in? If I don't get out of this soggy body bag I'm going to lose it and use this switchblade on somebody."

Not much later, having shucked the heavy Nomex flying suit, showered, and changed into his K2-B duty uniform— which was just an illegal older cotton flying suit—Captain Thibodeaux sat at a grey metal table in a grey metal straight back chair. His chair was tilted back at a forty-or-so degree angle. He had his boots, with nice dry cotton socks, on the corner of the table, feet crossed at the ankles. As he talked, his hands moved. Across from him sat an intelligence officer taking notes on the mission.

"We're at seventy-five hundred feet, per the frag order, tracking northbound in the middle of the Tonle Sap. By the way, who the hell at headquarters frags a refueling at optimum height for anti-aircraft guns?

"King 32 is passing gas," he continued, referring to the refueling tanker. "Anyway, so I put Jolly 53 on the hose first, because I wanted him done and headed back here before sunset. I didn't want a newly minted aircraft commander having to negotiate the storms along the border after dark. He took his gas and had just cleared the horizon headed home. I moved us into the contact position,"—here Thibodeaux's hands flattened out indicating one aircraft slightly behind and to the left of another— "and then hit the basket and moved up into the refueling position. We've got fuel flowing and everything is as it should be. Stretch has got Radio Australia tuned in on the HF, and we're listening to a fifties' tune—something like Be Bopaloola. You know, like on Bandstand…I give it a sixty-five, good for listening but hard to dance to." He looked across at the intel officer furiously scribbling away.

"Hey, you don't write things like that down. That's just-between-us kind of stuff. Headquarters will get all tangled up if we put in our reports that we listen to the radio while refueling. They know we do it, but we don't admit to it." He looked at the intel officer. "I take it you're new. Don't worry, you'll get the hang of it. Just relax for now, and I'll kind of give you hand signals about what you need to write down." Even though Thibodeaux was still so mad he would gladly have bitten the head off any outsider who happened to infringe upon squadron spaces during the next few hours, he realized there was no need to jump on someone who was obviously a newly arrived lieutenant. "It's probably the kid's first time away from home as an adult," he thought to himself.

"We get about five hundred pounds in the tanks when this eighty-five shell explodes at the one o'clock about three thousand feet above us. Well, I sit up a little taller and start to back off the hose per protocol. The AC— that's aircraft commander—" he said, looking at the kid across the table from him, "anyway, the AC on King is screaming, 'GROUND FIRE! BREAK AWAY, BREAK AWAY, BREAK AWAY!' I see his flaps start up and can hear him cob the power to the engines as he starts a significant pull up. Then I hear him on the radio yelling, 'TURNING LEFT!' He wants to turn away from the gun."

The debriefing officer had his hand up as if he wanted to ask a question. "Yes?"

"How did you know it was an eighty-five? Why not a thirty-seven or some other caliber?"

"Orange burst, grey-black smoke. So, as I was saying, the C-130 wanted to turn left. That was fine with me since I was ninety degrees off on a wing diving for the lake. I pulled the mike button and told him I was clear. The C-130 crew is all over Guard channel yelling, 'MAYDAY! MAYDAY! MAYDAY! KING 32, WE'RE TAKING ANTI-AIRCRAFT FIRE OVER THE TONLE SAP!' I didn't see any need to add to that since as soon as I got low enough we were going to water ski ourselves out of the area and back to channel eighty-seven. Channel eighty-seven—that's the navigation aide identifier for Nakhon Phanom—this 'Naked Fanny' place we call home."

Thibodeaux looked at the youngster and wondered if he shaved yet. An onlooker would have noticed that the captain looked no older than the debriefer, since Jean-Louis himself had only recently turned twenty-five.

"So, anyway, Stretch saw him first and yelled, 'Jesus Christ! They're bailing out!' I looked over and up to the left, and sure enough, here comes somebody out of the back of the C-130. He's falling. About that time another shell explodes out in front of us, but it's off a couple of thousand feet up and as much over to the right—nowhere near us or the C-130. Well, as you know, time slows down in those situations. I continue downward, heading for the water, and we're watching this guy fall. He pops his chute way too high, and now the wind's got him and he's drifting over towards Siam Reap—which is where we think the gun is."

"Ahhh...why did you think the gun was in Siam Reap?" The lieutenant had his hand up again.

"Put your goddamn hand down. This isn't Combat 101 class at the Academy." *Or maybe it is,* Thibodeaux thought. "Wasn't it you or one of your buddies who told us earlier this week that the Khmer communist groups were operating in and around Siam Reap? We've had some problems with North Vietnamese regulars over in the Parrot's Beak, so I assume they may have come as far west as Siam Reap— probably with the blessing of the local communists. Besides, the eighty-five is a towed weapon, and there aren't any other roads in the area."

"Oh...makes sense." The lieutenant added to his notes.

"So, the wind has got this guy and he's booking towards the east side of the lake. Nobody else ever came out of the C-130—which by now is almost out of sight. I get on the radio and ask King if he ordered a bail out. The aircraft commander sounded almost offended—didn't you think so, Stretch?" He turned his head to look at his copilot who was draped over the arms of some very uncomfortable aluminum tube and Naugahyde vinyl furniture.

Stretch moved his frame somewhat lugubriously, one leg coming down off the couch, the other going up. "Oh, without question. Kind of like...'How dare you call me a coward, sir?! Why my great granddaddy fought at Chickamauga and I myself have just cheated death at the hands of those damned Yankees—no wait, we're the Yankees now. Well still, any further besmirching of my family honor and I'll be forced to offer you choice of weapons.'"

"Huh?" The debriefer looked puzzled.

"Yes. Yes, he did. He sounded offended," continued Thibodeaux. "Almost like he thought I was challenging him to a duel or something....but then I said, 'So are you missing anybody?'

"After about thirty seconds I hear this...'Ahhhh...my flight engineer doesn't appear to be with us at this time.' So I punch the mike and ask, 'Could that be because he's on a nylon escalator heading toward Siam Reap?' Well, if silence can be expressive, the silence of that aircraft commander could have been an entire scene in Shakespeare.

"So, no big deal, right? The guy's going to come down in the water and we'll be on top of him as he does. He'll get out of his chute and we'll pick him up. No harm, no foul, so to speak. Then out of nowhere we hear on Guard channel, 'This is Blue

Chip. All aircraft avoid the Tonle Sap. I say again. All aircraft avoid the entire of the Tonle Sap.'

"Well, that's normal enough. Seventh Air Force doesn't want its birds to be shot at by a previously unknown fowling piece, so probably a good idea. Then I hear, 'Jolly Green 47, Blue Chip.'

"'Roger Blue Chip, go,' I reply.

"'Roger Jolly 47, Blue Chip. Assume you're en route channel eighty-seven?'

"'Ah, that's a negative Blue Chip. King 32 lost a crewmember who shortly is going to be in the water and we're making our way over to pick him up.' They hadn't heard the earlier conversation because I used Rescue discreet channel to talk to the King Bird.

"'Jolly 47, this is Blue Chip controller. Blue Chip directs Jolly 47 depart the area until Blue Chip can identify and organize an air strike against the threat.'

"'Roger Blue Chip. Understand. Jolly 47 will depart the area as soon as we pick up the survivor in the water.'

"'Negative, Jolly 47. Blue Chip is directing Jolly 47 depart area immediately. Other rescue elements will be directed to area later to effect rescue.'"

Thibodeaux lifted his left boot off his right ankle, put it on the table and crossed his left ankle with his right boot. "So, while we're having this delightful conversation we're getting nearer to where our boy is going to splash down and we can see some boats in the water headed for where they think he's going to come down. They're like small patrol boats. A little bigger than a Boston Whaler with a small wheelhouse and what looks to be a 12.7 mounted in the front. Thought they might be friendlies until they started shooting at us. So I tell the guys to unlimber our minis.

"Then Blue Chip is on the air again, 'Jolly 47 confirm receipt of order to leave area.'

"'Blue Chip, stay off the radio. We're under fire, engaging hostiles, and prosecuting a rescue.'

"I thought that was pretty clear. We had all three guns ready, so I told Jésus we'd take them down the right side first since that side has a wider field of fire, and then the stinger in the tail could get them as we passed by. I really don't think they were prepared for a helicopter that could shoot at them. When the stream of rounds from our number two mini-gun started splashing towards the bow, everyone on the boat froze. The gunner stopped firing and just looked at us. Then, when we walked that first stream through the boat, half of them dove overboard and the other half ducked under the gunwales. When we passed, we hit them with the number three gun from the tail, raking the boat from the bow to the stern, and obviously hitting either the engine or fuel line because the boat started burning, and the rest of them dove overboard.

"Just as I was turning towards the second boat I hear, 'Jolly 47, this is Blue Chip Controller Brigadier General Warren...' Stretch, what did he say his last name was?"

Before Stretch could answer, Schaffer moaned out, "Williamson," again running his hand from his forehead to his chin.

"That's right," the captain said, "Williamson."

"'I'm ordering you to disengage and leave the area immediately. Do you understand the meaning of a direct order?'

"So the second boat is shooting at us and a couple of rounds hit the left sponson tank with some significant thuds. Made you mad, Stretch. Didn't it?"

"Fucking A, it did." Which was about as succinctly eloquent as Stretch's Air Force Academy English got.

"Now we're about to take on the second boat which decides to zigzag, so I hit the mike switch and answer Blue Chip. 'Do you know what stay the fuck off the radio means? I'm in the middle of a rescue.'

"Their boat was doing a zigzag, which didn't mean we couldn't hit them, just that their gunner was having a hell of a time trying to hit us. I put the boat straight in front of us and pedal-turned right and left, allowing both the number one and number two guns to fire to the front. Both of them walked their rounds right into the bow of the boat and, just like with the first one, half the crew abandoned ship and the other half was ducking for cover. Again the old tail stinger convinced the rest of the crew to go overboard.

"By this time the flight engineer from the C-130 was in the water. Looked like he might be having a problem disengaging from his chute, so I hovered off to the downwind side, and put the number one PJ into the water. After a couple of minutes, he got the guy disengaged and clear of the chute. We put the hoist down from a fifteen-foot hover, winched the two of them up, and headed for Ubon to drop the flight engineer off with his brother C-130 types. We took on some fuel there since we only got five hundred pounds off the King bird, and came home. End of story. You get that?"

Thibodeaux looked at the intelligence officer. "Type it up, I'll sign it."

Sergeant Fisher, one of the administrative officers, appeared at the door to the briefing room with two other sergeants in tow. They were wearing side arms and armbands that identified them as security policemen.

"Sir, two sergeants from the Security Police."

The two sergeants came to attention. One said, "Sir, we're looking for Captain Thibodeaux. We have an order from the base commander to place him under arrest."

The squadron commander ran his hand yet again over his face and then pointed to Thibodeaux, still leaning back in the chair.

"Where's your officer?" Thibodeaux asked.

"Officer?" the sergeant asked.

"Officer," Captain Jean-Louis Thibodeaux answered. "I'm a captain in the regular United States Air Force. I am not a reservist. If you're going to arrest me, you must have an officer with you who has a written order from a senior officer who has court martial convening authority. Do you have a written order?"

"No, sir. We were instructed by our watch commander to come here and place you under arrest, and bring you to base headquarters on the orders of the base commander."

"Well, Sergeant, it appears neither your watch commander nor the base commander is acquainted with military custom and law, so I suggest you return and educate them. When arresting a regular officer, you require a written order from a senior officer who has the authority to convene a court martial, and that order must be delivered by a commissioned officer of equal or greater rank to the officer being arrested. So don't come back with a lieutenant. In fact, don't come back here at all. In about twenty minutes I'm leaving here for the Officers Club where I intend to have several shots of Mr. Jim's finest. Then I will be in my hooch—name's on the door—in the Valley of the Jolly Green Giants. Run along now, like good lads."

The sergeants looked at the squadron commander who nodded his head toward the door and said, "I guess he's right. He's never been wrong before, so I suggest you return to your watch commander and deliver the message. If you like, I'll call him to confirm."

"Thank you, sir. I would appreciate that very much since I doubt he'll believe me. He's a mustang, sir, you know, promoted from the ranks. I don't think he knows much about protocol and such."

No sooner had the sergeants departed than Captain Thibodeaux swung his feet to the floor and grabbed for the telephone. He dialed a series of numbers and, when the call was answered, said, "Can you establish a radio link with Seventh Air Force at Ton San Nhut Air Force Base, please? I want a line into the commander's office. I want to speak with Captain Jay Forrest. He's the commanding general's *aide-de-camp*. Please patch through to this line when you've got the link."

He turned to Schaffer. "Jay and I went to college together. He's a couple of years older and much more politically correct. He can charm a possum out of a tree and into a boiling pot."

The mental image of an opossum being charmed into a cooking pot was too much for the colonel. He pushed Stretch's lanky legs aside and plunked down on the Naugahyde. The cushion expelled its air in a long sigh, reinforcing the dank, mildewy smell of the wet, slowly rotting, plywood building.

While waiting on the call, Captain Thibodeaux left the room and went down the hall to an office with a sign on the door that read "Assistant Operations Officer." He opened a lower desk drawer, took out a bottle of Jim Beam bourbon, and, putting three shot glasses over his fingers, walked back to the briefing room. Putting the glasses on the table, he pulled the cork from the bottle and filled each of the shot glasses. He handed one to Stretch, one to Schaffer and, taking the last himself, raised it and offered the observation, "Life's a bitch and then you die." He downed the shot and poured himself another one.

The phone rang and, after going through the formalities of establishing a radio-to-telephone contact, he listened…and listened…and listened. Finally, after it seemed he would never get to say his piece, he started:

"Well, it's nice to hear from you, too, Jay. Look, it isn't all that bad. And to answer your question, yes, I do intend for you to save my tail. What are friends for? As for your other question, yes, I did know we were on Guard channel, but Jay, consider this. Didn't the Brigadier violate radio protocols by using his name on the radio? Didn't he assume an authority he didn't have, and thus again violate protocol and regulations by issuing what essentially was an illegal order? Isn't issuing an illegal order in and of itself illegal? Did he bother to tell the commanding general about the communist boats that fired on us and would have taken the flight engineer prisoner if we had waited for other forces to arrive? Did he mention his bird was somewhere over South Vietnam while he was attempting to orchestrate an event in Cambodia? Over."

He had finished his opening foray and, in accordance with the niceties of radio-telephone conversations, had offered the mike to the other side.

He listened briefly, and then said:

"Absolutely, without a doubt. The guy would probably already have a nail in his forehead since I doubt the North Vietnamese are taking prisoners if they're moving heavy stuff forward. You should have someone talk to him. He saw most of the engagement from his parachute. Over."

Another set of questions came from the other side.

"He didn't have his harness connected. He was moving from the front to the back to check that they weren't leaking any fuel from the tanks as they refueled us. That's when the gun opened up and his aircraft commander threw the aircraft into a steep climb. He went tumbling out the back. Not his fault, not the AC's fault. It just happened. Only way to prevent it would have been to close the ramp, and you know none of the crew wants a closed ramp when they're refueling a helicopter twenty feet off the horizontal stabilizer. Over."

After a few seconds, Thibodeaux concluded, "Well, listen, I got these people over here all hot and bothered to arrest me on the brigadier's authority. I ran them off the first time with some hooey about regular officers and convening authorities, but when they find out they've been hornswoggled they're going to be mad, so if you could do something quick...I'll buy the barbeque at the next Founder's Day reunion. Over."

After what sounded to those listening at a distance to be yet another tail-flaming fusillade, Thibodeaux replied, "Roger, understand. Thanks, Jay, I guess I owe you, but listen—you tell that Brigadier..."

At this the squadron commander grabbed the phone and said, "Captain Forrest, this is Lieutenant Colonel Schaffer. If I'm hearing the one side of this conversation correctly, I owe you a big one. He can be a real pain in the ass, but he's the best pilot I've got. So thanks. Over and out."

"Problem solved." Captain Thibodeaux said as he poured another round. "To friends!" He lifted his glass.

"To friends," echoed Shaffer.

"That's right," said Stretch, raising himself off the sofa to his full six foot seven inches.

"Friends. To us and those like us!"

"Damned few left!" said Thibodeaux.

"Amen!" said Shaffer.

CHAPTER 8

OVER THE TOP

THE ARMORY CLERK LAID THE CAR-15 on the counter and waited for the captain to sign for it before pushing it forward. The captain picked it up, slung it over his shoulder, and walked out of the armory. The clerk turned to his colleague who was seated at a desk behind the counter. "He's got a revolver he never takes out of the armory. And why doesn't he ask for additional clips of ammo like a lot of those guys do?"

The second clerk, without looking up, answered, "Probably because he doesn't even use the CAR. I don't think it's ever been fired. We keep it clean and he takes it out, but I think it goes somewhere in the gun box on his aircraft. And then after three days he brings it back. As for that revolver, the only time it was ever off the hook was when I brought it out so he could check the serial number when I issued it to him. That's Captain Thibodeaux. About nine months ago I helped him clean a Browning Hi Power 9 millimeter semi-auto. He didn't show me at the time, but the pistol was fitted with a barrel that allowed for attaching a suppressor."

"A suppressor? Aren't those against the Geneva Convention?"

"Absolutely. So I asked him about it and he said, 'I'm not saying I carry a suppressor, and I'm not saying I don't, but let me ask you two questions. First, if you were shot down over hostile territory would you rather have a revolver with six rounds, or a semi-automatic with fourteen rounds? Second, if you were hiding under a bush and a guy found you and you had to shoot him, would you rather do it with a revolver that sounds like a cannon and announces your presence to everybody within a mile, or would you rather engage him with a suppressed semi, so that only someone within a few meters would hear it?'

"So I thought about it a minute and agreed that I would like fourteen rounds and the suppressed semi, but then I said again that a suppressor is illegal according to the Geneva Convention. I found his reply very interesting. He said, 'I'd rather be tried by a court in The Hague, than hung by my thumbs in Hanoi.' So, my guess on the pistol is that he has his own; and, as for the CAR, I know the Jolly Greens carry captured AK-47s in their aircraft as well as Winchester assault shotguns. I've seen pictures of the PJs with bandoliers of twelve gauge shells, and I've heard stories of how when they go down on the jungle penetrator they immediately pepper the jungle with buckshot in all directions, just to ensure there's nobody waiting to jump out from under a bush. Does that answer your question?"

"Well, yes," answered the first armorer, "but still, where did he get a Browning with a suppressor?"

"My guess," said the second—only now looking up—"is that he got it from a Navy or Marine Corps pilot. Those guys can get whatever they want in the Philippines and take it on board their carriers. When one of them gets shot down and gets rescued by a Jolly, I'm sure they're willing to gift most anything to the pilot that plucks them out of the jungle. I had a guy in Saigon tell me lots of Navy guys have suppressors."

"So what happens if he gets caught with the semi and the AK?"

"Haven't the faintest idea and don't care. As long as we have the weapons we're supposed to have hanging on hooks in the back—and signatures for the ones that aren't there—we're good. And that's all I'm looking for on this tour. And that's all you should be looking for as well. By the way, I wouldn't go talking to people in the barracks or chow hall about guys not taking their weapons out of the armory, or having their own. If you do, the next thing is you'll be sitting in the Office of Special Investigations being interrogated, and you don't want that. There's lots of things that happen around here that you should just not talk about."

"Like what?" asked the newly arrived clerk.

"Like what we just talked about," said the second. "If the captain doesn't choose to take his revolver out of the armory it isn't any of my business, and it certainly isn't any of yours."

Jean-Louis put the CAR-15 in the gun box with the other weapons, ensuring the small piece of green tape was still on the butt so he could distinguish it from the other CARs there. His was the last, so the senior PJ reached down and locked the box, securing the weapons.

After he had climbed into the aircraft commander's seat, he and Stretch went through the run-up and shutdown checklists. Then they went through the cocking checklist. The aircraft was left in the cocked position, ensuring that if they had to quickly respond to an emergency call they could be airborne in two to three minutes—instead of the normal fifteen minutes a standard preflight, engine start, and prior-to-taxi procedure required. Because of the weapons in the gun box and the fact that the aircraft was now armed with three 7.62 millimeter GE electric mini-guns and twelve thousand rounds of ammunition, there would be armed guards around the aircraft for the next seventy-two hours—or until the aircraft departed the base, whichever came first.

Thibodeaux and his crew, having already briefed in the squadron ready room, broke to attend to their normal duties. Jean-Louis went to the office he shared with the other assistant operations officer, Stretch to his office as the squadron's classified materials officer, the senior PJ to the squadron's second building which housed PJ operations, Jésus to the maintenance hangar, and the junior PJ to the training room where he was reviewing Rescue manuals for his periodic flight crew check—which was due before the end of the month.

A second Jolly crew had completed an identical run-up and cocking checklist for their aircraft and, should a rescue scenario develop, would deploy as high bird, or backup, to the primary, or low bird, which was Captain Thibodeaux's aircraft. Should Captain Thibodeaux's crew or aircraft not be able to carry through with the mission, the second aircraft, under the command of recently promoted Captain Balboni, would make the rescue. After prepping their aircraft, Captain Balboni's crew had returned to their normal duties as well.

This was what the Jolly Green Giants did, day in and day out. They prepped for rescue missions. The squadron had flown more than a few of them during the past month, and talk was that the increasing number of rescues meant either that they would once again be deploying to Lima sites in the Laotian jungles—where they would be much closer to potential targets in North Vietnam—or, that they would commence "duckbutt" orbits over northern Laos—waiting aloft and refueling from their C-130 support aircraft, call sign King. For some reason, the C-130's call sign had recently been changed. It had been Crown, but now it was King. No one ever told you *why* something was done, only that it *was* done.

The squadron had recently received a shipment of updated tactical pilotage charts for northern Laos and southern North Vietnam. The fact that these charts had been received was known only to a few members of the squadron, but Captain Thibodeaux and Captain Balboni, the squadron publications officer, were among those few. Both of these officers had already replaced the maps in their respective map kits with the updated maps. It was the intention of the squadron commander to replace each crew's maps with the new versions as that crew rotated through the alert schedule. Thus, in seventy-two hours, two more crews would receive the new maps and the related briefing regarding new threats or obstructions noted on the maps. They would also receive plastic overlays printed with a classified grid that allowed crews to discuss coordinates on the maps without using the standard longitude and latitude markings. This made communication over unencrypted radio much easier.

So, Jolly Green 47 and her crew were prepared when the radio alarm sounded. As always, when the alarm sounded, the Jollys had no idea of where they were going, only that they were going. The crew jumped into the back of their alert vehicle and went roaring down the perforated steel planking to their aircraft. As they approached the aircraft, the radio crackled again, "Jolly Green 47, three five zero off of channel eighty-seven." They had their initial heading.

The ground crew had already pulled the tie downs and gear pins, the fire extinguishers were in place, and the fireguard was standing by. Stretch went in first, hitting the start handle for the auxiliary power plant. Thibodeaux followed, strapping himself into his seat while Stretch pushed the start switch for the number one engine. Strapped in, Jean-Louis reached up to start the number two engine while Stretch strapped in. Both engines on line, Thibodeaux keyed his microphone and requested permission for taxi and takeoff clearance.

"NKP Tower, Jolly Green 47. Flight of two, taxi, request midfield departure to the north."

"All aircraft, this is NKP tower. Hold your positions. Jolly Green scramble in progress. Jolly 47 cleared taxi and midfield departure to the north. Altimeter two niner eight niner. Winds three four five at five gust ten."

"Two niner eight niner. Jolly 47. Jolly 51, you ready?"

"Jolly 51. Roger that."

The two Jollys came out of their parking revetments, Jolly 51 following Jolly 47. As they reached the middle of the taxiway they turned left and lifted to a fifteen-foot hover. Nosing over, Jolly 47 went first, followed closely by Jolly 51. Beginning their climb, Jolly 47 turned to the north to intercept the 350-degree radial outbound off the NKP TACAN. As he did so, he radioed NKP tower, "Jolly Green flight airborne at 1215 local. Mission begins."

Thibodeaux called for the gear-up-after-takeoff checklist and checked in with the command post. "Joker, Jolly 47. Mission details?"

"Roger, Jolly 47. Joker. Mission details follow. Marine Corps H-46—call sign Awash 06—down at map coordinates Crab 21 Alpha 2. Eight souls on board. Enemy fire reported in area. Nail 22 en route to assess situation. Sandy 1-1, flight of four, en route from Takhli to support. Hold short of objective at Angels seven point five, repeat seven point five."

Stretch pulled the map from the briefcase, placed the acetate overlay on it, and found Crab 21 Alpha 2. "Crab 21" referred to one of the large blocks and "Alpha 2" to a smaller box within the larger block. "Not good, Kimosabe," he said, pointing to a spot on the map that was heavily forested but, more importantly, within the steep karst mountains of northeast Laos.

The vertical mountainsides made flying difficult for a variety of reasons. Winds swirling from every direction, sheer cliffs, and heavy vegetation that hid all manner of anti-aircraft weapons made this region almost as dangerous as it was near Hanoi in the area known as Route Pak Six. Still, difficult flying was what they did—and they were very good at it.

It would take almost two hours to reach the objective area so the crew settled in, doing the necessary checks and listening to the radio as Nail 22 began talking to the survivors on Guard channel. After about half an hour, Nail 22 had located the downed aircraft and passed more precise information to the rescue team. The information was not good. The H-46 was down in a small valley almost completely surrounded by steep cliffs, some reaching up to five thousand feet. If you didn't come in the way the H-46 had—by auto-rotating into the middle—the only other option was through a steep-sided canyon with a stream running through it. It was about two miles long and approached the valley from the east. The sides were close together and rugged. They could hide most any manner of threat from both the Nail forward air controller and the Sandy attack aircraft. A Jolly attempting to make an approach down the valley would subject itself to possible heavy fire from close-in weapons, and a Jolly attempting to make a steep approach to the valley would be a sitting duck while it slowly descended the two thousand feet between the top of the mountains and the valley floor.

Awash 06 reported sighting numerous hostiles in the area on his way down. Also, Awash 06 reported he and the others with him were all injured in some manner, and would require support getting into a rescue bird.

While this discussion was taking place, the A-1 Sandys arrived overhead and, with the guidance of Nail, began dragging the valley and canyon for ground fire. Neither the Sandys nor the Nail could actually get into either the canyon or the valley, and they could see very little since the valley was completely covered in ten-foot-high elephant grass. The walls were too steep and narrow in the canyon, and the valley was too small, for the fixed wing aircraft to maneuver. So they flew overhead. Nail 22 thought he saw some activity through the jungle canopy but wasn't sure. Sandy Lead didn't see anything in the canyon, but was fairly sure there were bad guys in the valley. He set up a steep dive angle and loosed off a couple of small rockets to the east of the downed H-46, but did not succeed in drawing any return fire that could help pinpoint hostile locations.

At that point it became Jolly's decision. Would they go down the canyon into the valley and return with the crew of Awash 06? There was the possibility that there were only a few lightly armed hostiles in the area. There was also the possibility that the hostiles Awash 06 had seen on his way down had not yet moved in to capture the crew because they were waiting on a rescue effort and had set a trap.

Thibodeaux's father had always said, "Prepare for the worst, expect the best, and deal with what you get." That meant he should expect that he was flying into a trap and conduct himself accordingly. There was never a possibility that they would not attempt the rescue because they were, after all, the Jolly Greens—the premier rescue force in the history of military aviation. "That Others May Live" might have seemed only a motto to some, but to Thibodeaux and his crew it was the *raison d'etre*. Still, foolhardiness was foolhardiness, and going into this situation, as it was presented, seemed foolhardy.

"Man," Stretch said, "I'm not real sure about getting in through that canyon."

"It's not getting in I'm worried about," Thibodeaux mused. "I know how to get in. It's getting out that worries me."

"And just how do you propose we get in?" Stretch asked.

"We'll go in over the top," the captain replied.

"Oh, of course. Over the top," Stretch repeated, knowing he didn't really understand. But if Thibodeaux seemed unconcerned, then he was unconcerned; or at least he would seem so to the crew, all of whom were listening on the intercom.

It took Thibodeaux about a minute to make his decision. "All rescue aircraft go pistol," he transmitted.

Pistol was a revolving radio frequency that changed daily so that rescue aircraft could communicate with each other in the clear, even if the bad guys were listening to the normal frequencies used by the teams. You couldn't use the frequency for extended conversations, but you could have short, concise conversations before the scanners could find the frequency you were using.

"Sandy's up." "Jolly 51's up." "Nail's up." "King's up." All the aircraft checked in.

"This is Jolly 47. Here's the plan. Nail 22 will ascertain from Awash 06 what altimeter setting he was using when he was hit and, if possible, what his altimeter is reading in the valley. Jolly 47 will be listening. At fifteen past the hour, the Sandys will make a pass down the canyon, putting in some rockets and hosing down whatever they can reach with their wing guns. They'll shoot up the valley as best possible. At sixteen past the hour, Nail 22 will tell Awash 06 to stand by for rescue. Jolly 51 will let down and make a run at the mouth of the canyon, turning away just before entering. During that time Jolly 47 will be approaching the valley from the northwest, and will let down into the valley to load the survivors. As Jolly 47 is loading survivors, King will call in some fast movers to expend on the canyon. Shortly after that, Jolly 47 will come down the valley with the survivors on board. The Sandys will support from overhead as best possible. King, do you have fast movers on standby?"

"Roger, Jolly 47. King has a flight of F-105s with CBU— cluster bomb units—standing by."

"No napalm, King?"

"Nope. Just CBU."

"Roger, understand CBUs. It'll have to do. Jolly 47 will call for fast movers when we have half the survivors on board. Questions?"

There being no questions, the aircraft returned to their primary frequencies, and Nail contacted Awash 06 on Guard channel. The Awash 06 aircraft commander was in some pain, but his copilot was more coherent, and gave Nail his best estimates on both the questions.

King, using another discreet frequency, briefed the F-105 flight commander on his target and timing. Nail 22 would show the F-105s the way to the canyon.

Sandy Lead, using his squadron's discreet frequency, instructed his flight on sequence of approach, weapons, and targets.

Thibodeaux reached up and reset his altimeter to the barometric setting the Awash 06 copilot provided, instructing Stretch to do the same. He explained, "I want to be as close as possible to an accurate altimeter reading, and, since I don't think we've had a major change in barometric pressure, this is the best way I can think of to make sure we don't overshoot before we swap ends going into the valley. Remember, that bottom-mounted radar altimeter isn't going to do us any good."

Based on Thibodeaux's description, Stretch now knew what the plan would be. They had practiced it once or twice, scaring the daylights out of everyone except Thibodeaux. It was dangerous, but it just might keep them from being shot up on the way in. But they were still going to have to come through the canyon on the way out.

At fifteen past the hour, the Sandys rolled in on the canyon and began peppering it with rockets and their 20 millimeter wing guns. At sixteen past, Nail 22 transmitted, "Awash 06 stand by for rescue," and Jolly 51 headed for the mouth of the canyon. As Jolly 51 approached the entrance, tracer fire erupted from inside the canyon sending up a most unwelcoming display of fireworks. No question, it was a trap. Jolly 51 broke to the east, but as he did, two rounds ripped into his number one engine. Balboni's aircraft shuddered, but these were strongly built Sikorsky H-53s, and he completed his break away from the canyon. Still, he was now losing power on the number one engine and was of little use to anyone.

"King, Jolly 51. We're hit and having to shut down number one. We'll be heading home. Better launch the backup bird."

"Roger, Jolly 51. Understand you have combat damage and are returning to channel eighty-seven. We'll contact Joker and let them know. Will you need fuel?"

"King, Jolly 51. Negative at this time on the fuel. Unless we have fuel tank damage we don't know about, we should be able to make channel eighty-seven without fuel."

"Roger. Understand no fuel required this time. Safe flight home, 51."

While this was happening, the Sandys had reached the valley and had kicked up quite a bit of mud with their rockets and guns. If there were bad guys there, they had their heads buried pretty deep.

As fountains of mud and elephant grass rose into the air, Jolly 47's nose appeared over the top of the karst. As the fuselage cleared the ridge, Thibodeaux rolled the aircraft 90 degrees to the right and pushed it over, pointing the refueling probe directly at the ground. As he did so, in a very calm voice he said, "Copilot, call the altitude and rotor tach," and Jolly 47 began its two-thousand-foot dive into the valley. Thibodeaux spotted the H-46 and aimed his dive just to the east of the downed helicopter.

To stay on target, Thibodeaux rolled the aircraft around the refueling probe. One turn, two turns, three turns, four turns...

"One thousand feet, rotor in the green," Stretch called.

...five turns, six turns...

"Five hundred feet, rotor in the yellow."

Thibodeaux had no intention of pulling collective to slow the rotor because he was going to need the energy when he started his pullout.

"Two fifty, rotor in the red," Stretch grunted.

Thibodeaux stopped the rotation and pulled hard on the cyclic. The nose started to come up, the tail to go down. He sighted the downed H-46 out his chin bubble and started to pull the collective to put pitch in the blades and break his precipitous plunge. The valley floor closed at an alarming rate. His touchdown wasn't the smoothest, but nothing broke. In the back of his mind he was a little disappointed it wasn't a perfect landing, but the front of his brain was already instructing his flight engineer and the two pararescue jumpers to go, "Now!"

He had touched down with his tail to the H-46 so the survivors could be loaded from the ramp. Before coming over the ridge, he had instructed the PJs to load the survivors using shoulder drags rather than the Stokes litter, since the latter required two men to carry each survivor. He wanted the survivors brought up the ramp and placed on the floor. The crew had taken off their body armor and Thibodeaux had instructed that armor be placed on top of the survivors when they were taken on board.

It took about twenty seconds for the first round to hit the aircraft. It sounded like someone striking their aluminum skin with a ball-peen hammer—somewhat dull and metallic. Then another, and another. He instructed Stretch to get out of his seat and use first the number one, and then the number two mini-gun.

It took Stretch a few seconds to get out of his seat and parachute harness. Uncoiling his long legs took a mite longer, but within half a minute he was working one gun and then the other. The whine of the electrically operated GE Gatling guns, and the roar of the two thousand rounds a minute they were producing, seemed to slow the incoming fire.

Three survivors were on board almost immediately, then four. Thibodeaux watched in his mirror. Then Jésus fell as he neared the ramp of the aircraft while pulling another survivor by the shoulders of his fatigues. He rose to a kneeling position, holding his leg. Thibodeaux saw one of the PJs pick up the survivor first, ever true to Rescue's motto, and then return to help Jésus limp back onto the aircraft.

At that point Thibodeaux squeezed his mike trigger, "Nail, Jolly 47. Send in the fast movers."

Rounds continued to hit the aircraft, but his gauges still all showed green. He was thankful that the bad guys thought the wing tip sponson fuel tanks would explode if they shot them. They were like bullet magnets, taking many more hits than the rest of the aircraft. In fact, the tanks were now foam filled since he had transferred all fuel to his main tanks before commencing his dive. Still, he hoped Charlie—or whoever was shooting at them—wouldn't wise up to that fact and start shooting at something else.

Even over the whine of his own engines, Thibodeaux could hear the roar of the F-105s as they made their bombing runs on the canyon.

Stretch had turned his gun over to a limping Jésus and climbed back into his seat. Jésus, with a belt tourniquet on his right leg, had plugged into the intercom in the back and said, "We've got them all, let's get the hell out of here."

One PJ was putting the armor over the survivors who were lying down the center line of the aircraft floor. The other, slightly dragging his left leg, positioned himself in the gun tub on the ramp of the aircraft and began to spray 7.62 rounds into the elephant grass. Jésus stayed on the number two gun, attempting to protect Thibodeaux's side of the airplane.

Jolly 47's landing had placed the nose away from the canyon, and as Thibodeaux picked the aircraft up to a hover, he transmitted, "Bugler, sound the charge! Jolly's coming out!"

He didn't know why he said it. It just came out. Something about a charge down a valley and all that.

He made a pedal turn towards the canyon and, keeping the nose down in the elephant grass, began to accelerate. Rounds were hitting the aircraft from all sides. He called for gear up, and Stretch slapped the gear handle into the up position.

Thibodeaux didn't want the gear dragging in the trees, and it was his plan to spend the next few minutes in the trees—or even lower if he could get there. He also wanted to protect his gear in case he needed to make a roll-on landing later.

The second PJ, having secured the survivors, was now on the number one gun and all three minis whined and roared as three-foot jets of flame flickered from the six-barreled guns. Overhead, the Sandys fired rockets and guns in advance of Jolly 47 as the helicopter made its way to the canyon.

Just before entering the canyon, Thibodeaux felt the airplane shake violently, like a dog coming out of a lake. The number one engine's fire light illuminated.

"Fire light number one engine. Exhaust gas temperature confirms fire," Stretch reached for the number one fuel shutoff handle.

"Let it burn. We need the power." Thibodeaux ignored the checklist for engine fire.

"Approaching airspeed redline," Stretch said, as the airspeed indicator approached 170 knots.

"Roger," was all Thibodeaux said.

Thibodeaux held the airplane on the deck, as close as he could fly to the ground without running into it. The engines strained. As he went through 175 knots, the number one engine fire light went out. Without any conscious thought, he realized the wind velocity he had generated had probably blown out the fire. The number one engine power tachometer stabilized at 60 percent. At least he had some part of the engine, but without full power, the speed he needed wasn't going to be there. It had already begun to drop back through the red line to 170, then down to 160 and 150. One-and-a-half engines wasn't what he needed right now.

He could not dodge the ground fire by jinking the aircraft from side to side because the canyon wasn't wide enough. He stayed as low as he could. He saw people running out into the stream to shoot at him. He wished he had forward-firing weapons on board, but even without them he knew that these particular people would soon realize running out in front of a low flying helicopter wasn't the smartest thing they had ever done. He was flying so low he could almost skewer them on his refueling probe, and when he passed overhead the hundred-plus-mile-an-hour downwash from his rotors blew them down and rolled them over and over in the sharp rocks of the stream.

The canyon turned left ahead, and as he banked the aircraft into the turn, the copilot's plexiglass chin bubble shattered. Stretch slumped forward and then backward, ending up with his head hanging to the inside of the aircraft towards Thibodeaux. He tried to straighten himself, but seemed disoriented. His face had numerous small puncture wounds from pieces of plexiglass. Several of the gauges on his side of the cockpit were missing their glass, and the gauge indicators were bent outward. Something had hit the airplane hard.

Thibodeaux also had pieces of plexiglass in his neck, face, left arm, and thigh. The punctures felt like yellow jacket stings on a hot summer day—meaning they hurt like hell.

"PJ up front," Thibodeaux ordered. "Copilot's hit."

The number one PJ stepped up on the gun box and leaned into the cockpit to undo Stretch's harness. When he had the straps clear, he pulled Stretch over the radio console and into the back of the aircraft where he began a triage to evaluate the pilot's wounds. There was a considerable amount of blood, and the PJ couldn't tell whether it was all from the relatively superficial shrapnel wounds left by the plexiglass and instrument housing fragments, or if there was some type of a projectile wound as well. As the PJ leaned over Stretch, he could still hear the small arms rounds impacting the aircraft—even over the scream of the engine mounted just above his head. He worked quickly, checking each blood spot for its wound. There were literally hundreds. He left Stretch's helmet on after he had checked to make sure no blood was coming from underneath the now-cracked visor.

"He'll be glad of that," the PJ thought to himself. And then he thought, "If the captain gets hit, we'll all buy the farm today."

The H-46 copilot, who had a broken left arm, attempted to get up and go to the cockpit. He was in pain, but he thought he could help if they'd just let him into the cockpit. The PJ gently put him back on the floor, replaced the King Arthur armor on top of him, and gave him a shot of morphine.

Up front, Thibodeaux now felt and heard the roar of a 120-knot wind coming through the cockpit, but he could see the opening to the canyon. The Sandys roared overhead, starting a dive toward the opening. They fired all their remaining rockets, including those with white phosphorous anti-personnel warheads, which exploded in the air and rained hot white phosphorus down on those below.

"Jolly's coming up to the right," Thibodeaux radioed as the helicopter cleared the canyon and he began a climbing right-hand turn.

As he began the turn, he felt the controls buck twice, but he couldn't tell if it was a blade problem or a problem with the hydraulics. The kicking didn't recur, so he concentrated on taking up a heading for home and hoped he could climb above the small arms fire that followed him from near the canyon's mouth. At three thousand feet he took the time to scan his instruments. Those on the copilot's side were pretty much useless, but the performance gauges on his side of the aircraft were intact. His hydraulic pressure needles were jumping, which he didn't like, but what caught his eye immediately was his fuel state. He was low on gas, and the reading was too low to have been caused by usage. He had a hole somewhere in a main fuel tank. He needed fuel, but he also needed to be sure the fire was actually out in the number one engine. The EGT—exhaust gas temperature—gauge was indicating a yellow condition on the engine, but he had to be sure there was no fire. If there was, when he took on gas the spray from the nozzle would ignite and that would be that. All today's work would be for naught. He could shut the engine down, but it was a long way home on one engine. Still, he had little choice, so he reached up and pulled the engine throttle to the "Shut Off" position and the fuel shutoff handle to the "Off" position. That cut the fuel to the engine. By the time he reached the tanker the exhaust gas temperature would have to be down in the green range or he couldn't refuel. It was a certainty that after refueling, as he backed off the hose, the fuel nozzle would spray his aircraft before the spring-loaded refueling value closed. If that spray precipitated an explosion, he would take the C-130 down with him because he would only be fifty feet behind its wing when he unplugged.

With the number one engine shut down, his speed dropped even lower and the controls kicked again.

"Damn," he thought. "It's a blade damper, the hydraulics, or the automatic flight control system." None of those were really good thoughts at the moment. He knew he had to level off and take some pitch out of his blades. It looked like he would be going home at three thousand feet and one hundred ten knots.

"King 32, Jolly 47. Battle damage report."

"Jolly 47, King. Go."

"Jolly 47, thirteen souls on board, twelve wounded. Request emergency personnel meet aircraft. Number one engine shut down, losing fuel rapidly. Request Joker launch backup Jolly in case 47 must abort en route."

"Jolly 47, King. Transmit and hold for steer."

"Jolly 47, heading two zero five, altitude three thousand, indicating one hundred ten knots. Five, four, three, two, one, one, two, three, four, five. Jolly out."

"Roger, Jolly. We have you. Continue on current heading. King is on intercept course. Understand you're at three thousand. Can you make seven thousand?"

"King, Jolly. Doubtful seven thousand. Speed is dropping with altitude, and I don't think I can maintain over one hundred ten knots above three thousand."

Each member of the C-130 crew thought about descending into the small arms environment where a refueling operation required straight and level flight, making their aircraft a perfect target. No one wanted to do it, and each crewmember hoped the pilot would decline to take the aircraft down.

"Jolly 47, understand refueling altitude is three thousand feet at one hundred ten knots. Standby, we're en route."

As they heard their pilot's transmission, each member of the crew, suppressing a sigh, silently agreed with the aircraft commander's decision. How could they not hazard their aircraft? After all, they were Rescue, and part of the team. Still, they'd rather have been part of the team at ten thousand or eleven thousand feet.

Thibodeaux called Jésus into the cockpit to operate the refueling probe and tank switches. He planned to keep the fuel levels balanced in the two main tanks. He couldn't transfer any gas into the wing tanks because those tanks were now filled with foam that had expanded after the tanks had been struck by God-only-knew how many small arms rounds. Thibodeaux thought about jettisoning the wing tanks for more speed, but did not, preferring to retain the tanks as targets for hostile gunners. He could still drop them at any point, but he really wanted to take them back to base so he could see how many rounds they had stopped. Besides, while jettisoning the tanks might give him a couple of miles per hour, he now had the airplane in balance and dropping tanks could prove a risky move. If one of the latches didn't fully disengage, he would have a 450-gallon wing tank dangling on one side pulling him down. "Nope," he decided. "Better to stay with the devil you know."

Thibodeaux was concerned that his fuel quantity gauges were indicating a rapid loss of fuel. He pushed the reset button on the second hand of the eight-day clock as he noted how many pounds of fuel he had in both tanks. As he did so, the controls bucked again.

"Not a damper," Thibodeaux thought. "It's like I've got air in the hydraulic lines."

The indicators on his hydraulic gauges were vibrating in a disturbing manner. Loss of hydraulics was a bailout procedure, and he had eight survivors plus a disabled copilot who couldn't bail out. If the gauges began to fluctuate significantly, he would have to make an emergency landing somewhere, and at the moment he was still flying over heavily forested and mountainous terrain. He would be little better off than the H-46 had been. If, on the other hand, it was the AFCS—automatic flight control system—he could continue to fly the airplane, but it would be a real bear to do so. He would have to apply over 150 pounds of pressure to get the five-thousand-pound rotor head to move, and there was no "touch" flying with a failed AFCS. The airplane would lumber like a ship rolling in heavy seas.

He knew he should report the problem as an addendum to his combat damage report, but if he did, there would be no way King would let him get close enough to refuel. And he needed gas. He also knew he should put his gear down, but that would have slowed him even more, and he needed the speed he had if he hoped to keep up with the C-130 during refueling.

If his AFCS failed and he ran out of fuel, he knew he was going to be in one big world of hurt. A failed AFCS required a run-on landing since hovering without the AFCS was pretty much out of the question. Still, he thought if he could get near the Mekong, the land would be more level, and he might pull off a slide-on belly landing. He couldn't land it in the water. Sikorsky swore the airplane would float, but he knew his wouldn't—not with a missing chin bubble on the copilot's side and who-knew-how-many holes in the fuselage.

He looked at the fuel loss on the gauges and didn't even need to do the math. It was bad. He must have multiple holes in both of his tanks, meaning someone had been low enough to shoot directly upward at them while they were coming out of the canyon. This gave him cause for concern about the H-46 survivors in the back.

"Fred," he said addressing the senior PJ, "How are our passengers?"

Fred Sargent, known as Sergeant Sargent (because, well, he was—and one hell of a PJ too) responded, "No worse than when we loaded them, Captain. They have some fairly serious concussions, broken bones, contusions, and a few cuts from debris, but unless there are some serious internal injuries I'm not seeing, these guys will be out of the hospital before some of us are." He was looking at Stretch, whom he had placed in one of the litters attached to the wall of the aircraft and who remained unconscious.

The airplane bucked again just as Thibodeaux heard, "Jolly, King. Tally Ho. We have you in sight. Commencing a turn to place you on our left wing."

"Roger that, King. I have you level at my eleven o'clock." Thibodeaux could see the big aircraft silhouetted against the afternoon clouds.

King began a turn that took it behind Jolly 47 and brought it up on the Jolly's right side. As he drew into position off 47's wing he said, "King is at Jolly's three o'clock. King assumes lead. Jolly is cleared into pre-contact position." The C-130 was a little nose up and had its landing flaps deployed to enable it to fly as slowly as the Jolly.

"Roger. Understand cleared pre-contact."

Thibodeaux turned—or more appropriately, slid—Jolly 47 over to a position just below and to the left of the C-130. The refueling basket attached to the hose from the left refueling nacelle was making small circles just above and to the right of the Jolly's nose. Before sliding into the pre-contact position, Thibodeaux had asked Jésus to run out the refueling probe. This was essential because if the probe didn't deploy, the titanium-tipped rotor blades would chop the refueling hose into chunks.

"Works as advertised," he thought. "Now if the pilot can just work as advertised..."

With his fingertips on the top of the stick, he pulled it slightly to the rear and left while edging up on the collective in his left hand. He was now level with the refueling basket as it continued to make counterclockwise circles. He pulled up on the collective while pushing forward on the stick, and the probe caught the webbing on the basket and went forward. Thibodeaux could feel a satisfying click as the probe pushed the spring-loaded valve open.

"Contact left," he said as he pulled ever so slightly on the collective, and once again pushed the stick just barely to the left and rear. "Refueling position," he added, looking straight into the C-130's left wing fuel dump tube. He regulated his height by a reference to the larger airplane's wing flap and engine nacelle.

"Fuel flowing," transmitted the flight engineer on the King Bird.

Noting the fuel gauges, Thibodeaux turned his head to look at Jésus who was leaning into the cockpit while standing on the gun box just under the flight deck's door. The gauges didn't appear to be moving much. They indicated a slight increase, but not the dramatic upswing one normally got when taking on fuel.

"King, Jolly. Confirm rate of transfer."

"Roger, Jolly. Standard rate of transfer observed on King."

"Then King, we have a problem. We seem to be losing fuel at only a slightly slower rate than you are transferring."

"Roger, Jolly. We are observing a significant loss of fuel from your main tanks." The crew on King was looking through the side windows on a level with the Jolly.

"King, do you have sufficient fuel to tow Jolly 47 home?"

"Standby, Jolly."

This was the only alternative left for Thibodeaux. His aircraft was losing fuel at a rapid rate. Either he put down in hostile territory, risked capture, and forced deployment of another rescue mission, or he had to fly back to NKP on the hose of King 32.

"Jolly, King. At current transfer rate King has sufficient fuel to take Jolly within twenty-five nautical miles of destination as long as King also recovers there for refueling. Will that help?"

"King, Jolly. It will have to. Thanks."

Refueling was one of the touchiest of the things Jolly pilots did, and they were always glad to unplug. But now Thibodeaux would have to refuel for more than 130 miles—certainly the longest refueling run of anyone in the squadron these days. At his current speed, he would have to hang on for just over an hour. He relaxed and settled in as much as he could, given that he was hanging on a hose fifty feet off the wing of a C-130, and only about thirty feet from its horizontal stabilizer. A mistake here could kill both crews, but Thibodeaux was an acknowledged pro, and "Legs" Studeman, the King Bird's pilot, was determined that any failure would not be his.

Thibodeaux now watched the hydraulic gauges more closely than the fuel gauges. Although they vibrated, they were not fluctuating. To his dismay, about fifty miles from home, the AFCS light began to flicker on the segmented caution panel and then the master caution light came on. Thibodeaux was losing his AFCS, which was his link between his control inputs and forces delivered to the rotors. Without the AFCS, moving the controls required the arm and leg muscles of a weight lifter.

Stabilized in position, he could only hope they encountered no strong air pockets or other turbulence, and that King planned no turns. He held the controls tightly, his muscles tensed, ready to pull back on the stick and push downward on the collective to break the contact with the hose if necessary, and then clear the C-130 as expeditiously as possible. The possibility of a collision between the two aircraft had just increased exponentially.

Squeezing his mike trigger, Thibodeaux said, "King, Jolly. No turns please. Just take us as close to base as this heading will get us, and no questions, please."

The King aircraft commander suspected exactly what was going on and said to his copilot as he took the controls from him, "My aircraft. I suspect our friend just lost his AFCS." Then he spoke to his crew, "Keep a close watch to see if he starts to oscillate. If he does, we have no option but to call for a breakaway. If he doesn't, we'll keep him hooked up as long as possible."

Muscles tensed on the C-130, and everyone but the aircraft commander looked hard at Jolly 47. The aircraft commander flew the airplane straight and level, hoping he would hit no significant turbulence.

The copilot very thoughtfully noted, "Sir, if the Jolly lands first and can't clear the runway, we won't have anywhere to go."

"Right you are," replied Captain Studeman. "So, I guess we'll drop the Jolly at twenty-five miles, make a quick landing and get the hell off the runway. How are you on tactical approaches?"

"Oh, okay, I guess," the copilot answered. Captain Studeman seemed to be taking all this very calmly he thought.

In truth, Captain Studeman was very much concerned about his close friend, Captain Thibodeaux. They had been in the same pilot training class at Randolph Air Force Base four years earlier, and Thibodeaux had been a great help to Studeman in getting through T-38 formation flying. Thibodeaux had been the outstanding graduate of the class, and Studeman had very much appreciated the support Thibodeaux had offered on his behalf. He would get him as close to NKP as he could.

It always amazed Studeman just how small a world the Air Force was. Thibodeaux had gone off to fly fighters, Studeman had gone to tactical airlift, and they had both become aircraft commanders in Air Rescue. To date, twelve members of the class he and Thibodeaux had shared had been lost in combat and noncombat aircraft crashes. Studeman didn't want Thibodeaux to become number thirteen on the list. A small and dangerous world—that's what they had joined when they became pilots—a small and dangerous world. He asked his flight engineer for a fuel check.

"We're on target, but we'll need to make a beeline for the runway after we drop the Jolly, sir."

"Roger that."

He wondered just how much Thibodeaux was sweating, and looked over his left shoulder at the Jolly. While not rock solid, it wasn't showing the oscillation that heavy helicopters generally begin as their pilots fight to stabilize positions without AFCS.

At that point, the TACAN distance indicator rolled over to twenty-five. Legs keyed his microphone:

"Jolly, we're two five miles out. Disconnect. Good luck. We'll see you on the ground."

"Roger King. Thanks for the tow."

Thibodeaux pulled backward, the stick grasped firmly in his hand rather than just his fingers, as would have been the case if the AFCS was working. The Jolly slowed, and when the refueling probe came loose from the valve, a heavy mist of fuel sprayed over the helicopter. Long reconciled to ignoring things over which he had no control, Thibodeaux was more concerned with how long the fuel in his tanks would last. As he reached down and switched his UHF radio to the NKP tower frequency he heard King negotiating a tactical approach to the runway. King 32 would be fine.

He waited for King to get his instructions and then radioed:

"NKP tower, Jolly Green 47 is two two miles northeast field at three thousand declaring an emergency and requesting straight-in approach runway one four."

He went through the radio exchange necessary for declaring an emergency, and, as they went through ten miles, he sighted the field. "NKP tower, runway in sight."

At five miles he moved the gear handle to the down position. While it seemed to take longer than normal, he got three green lights for landing gear down and locked. He had practiced many AFCS-off landings, so he was only concerned that his gear wasn't flat. He didn't have time for another aircraft to check, so the status of the gear was his only unknown until...

At two miles out, the number two engine quit. He was out of fuel. He still had the roar of the wind through the broken chin bubble, but there was no whine from the engine.

"Jolly Green 47. Engine failure, number two engine. Jolly is dead stick," he radioed.

Still in his seat on King 32, Legs thought, "Oh, shit!" But at the same time, he was amazed at how calm Thibodeaux sounded as he made the pronouncement.

Thibodeaux pushed down on the collective, shifting the weight of his body to help stiff-arm the lever down. Then he pulled up slightly. Then he sat on the lever again. Then pulled up slightly. He was milking as much distance as he could get from his now auto-rotating helicopter. He couldn't afford to touch down in the overrun of the runway because it was lined with catch cables to stop tailhook-equipped fighters. He also couldn't assume a normal nose-up landing attitude because that would slow him. He held the nose slightly low, pushing harder than he wanted on the stick.

He was sure he was going to catch his gear on the cables in the overrun but, as he pulled up on the collective a final time, the airplane floated just slightly. The touchdown was a perfect three-point landing. It wasn't the recommended touchdown attitude, but Thibodeaux thought it might make up for the less-than-perfect landing in the valley. He waited for the ground loop that would follow if he had landed with flat tires on one or both sides, but it never came. The aircraft rolled straight down the middle of the runway.

He didn't attempt to brake the aircraft, not knowing the extent of the damage, but that wasn't important since he was at the very beginning of an eight-thousand-foot runway.

The aircraft stopped fifteen hundred feet down the runway—trailed by ambulances, fire engines, staff cars, and blue pickup trucks.

As he rolled to a stop, Thibodeaux automatically keyed his microphone before realizing that, with no engines and his rotor not turning, he had no electricity for the radios. Still, he looked at the eight-day clock and said to himself:

"Jolly 47, full stop, 1718 local time. Mission complete."

CHAPTER 9

ALMOST GOING HOME

THIBODEAUX LEANED OVER THE WASHBASIN, splashing the slowly running thin stream of hot water on his face. He felt the pressure building once more and blew his nose for the third time, yet again producing copious amounts of mucus from the right nostril.

"Damn!" he thought as he dabbed at his reddening nose with the washcloth. "Damn. Damn. Damn! I won't be able to fly until I beat this sinus infection." But then it struck him that not flying might not be a bad thing. "Stretch can take the crew on the black missions now that he's back on flying status and has been made an aircraft commander. And doing those duckbutt precautionary orbits over the Tonle Sap supporting the bombing in Cambodia doesn't thrill me. So, being DNIF for my last week or so in-country might be just fine."

The more he thought about remaining on the Duty Not Involving Flying list until he departed country, the less concern he felt. He would have to pass an annual flight physical at his next assignment anyway, so remaining DNIF for now wasn't necessarily a bad thing. He could sit in the sun and bake his sinuses—and there was nothing like the Thai sun for baking things. Besides, he didn't have to report to his next assignment for almost two months. He would be taking his leave in Beirut, Rome, and Paris to practice the languages he hadn't spoken frequently since college. It would be good to get away from the Air Force for a while. The past few months had been difficult. He'd had to take on a new copilot and train him for the black missions, and, while he had handpicked the best of those available, the new guy was no Stretch.

As he leaned over the basin again, he thought of all that had happened during the past year. It made his head hurt. Well, to be fair, maybe it was the sinus infection rather than the past year's events that made his head hurt. "Still," he mused, "it might be a good time to start a journal." But then, as he always did when considering a journal, he discarded the prospect as being without merit. He didn't keep a journal because he didn't want anyone asking to see it, particularly if someone, sometime in the future, was unhappy with something he had done. He also did not keep a journal because, while he had never actually broken regulations, he had bent them an awful lot. He believed in pushing the edges of the envelope just as far as they would go. He had always had a good reason for pushing those edges—well, almost always— although once or twice the reason had been just to see where the corners of the envelope were.

He looked hard at himself in the mirror. "My God," he thought. "I look forty years old." It was his eyes. They looked tired.

"It's just the damned infection," he rationalized. He rejected that he could have aged significantly in just one year, although...

The squadron had changed a lot in that year. Schaffer was gone, replaced by Lieutenant Colonel Abruzzi who, like Schaffer, understood how to command. However, the new operations officer, Major Dynia, was a real stickler for regulations and a very bad pilot. He avoided flying whenever he could and had not yet been certified as an aircraft commander. Given the current feeling of the standardization pilot, Major Dynia would never be certified. The major could, however, make life miserable on the ground. He had come in with a big fire in his stomach—a strong desire to lead a heroic bunch of pilots—but alas for him, the glory days were past. It was as if he had come late to a dance and the orchestra was already playing *Good Night Ladies*.

But it was like that all over the base. The war had officially ended in January with the signing of the Paris Peace Accords. That, of course, was the war in Vietnam; decidedly not the war in Laos or Cambodia where daily combat missions were still being flown in an attempt to blunt pushes by the Pathet Lao and the Khmer Rouge communist groups still trying to oust the current and legitimate governments. In addition, the CIA had not stopped its black missions into North Vietnam where they continued searching for small camps where still-missing prisoners of war might be kept. So, although there were no aircraft going "downtown" to bomb Hanoi and Haiphong, and there were no more truck interdictions along the Ho Chi Minh Trail, the special operations covert war was still very hot.

Because the war was officially over, all commanders on the base—except those who commanded Rescue operations—had reverted to peacetime procedures. No more fatigues in the office. Flight suits only on the flight line—definitely not in the officers' club, even though the plywood flooring of that club still squished water up between joints as you walked on it. Of course, shoes and boots had to be polished, and no handlebar moustaches or beards were permitted. No sidearms could be carried, and, most important of all, haircuts had to be regulation. In most ways, it was like somebody had pushed a 1960 reset button. It was amazing to remember how much paperwork had to be done in the peacetime Air Force. It was paperwork that, somehow, had never needed to be done when people were flying and dying.

Of all the combat units left on the base, only the Jolly Greens were still active. Every other unit had dropped back into a training mode. The Jollys continued to fly precautionary orbits over Cambodia in case a B-52 crew had to bail out. So far, none had, and it was very unlikely they ever would.

It had become much harder to hide the covert night operations flights within the much-diminished activity level, but thankfully, this would not be Thibodeaux's problem as soon as he went up to flight ops and reported himself DNIF.

He picked up the freshly starched and pressed khaki uniform shirt—knowing full well it would look like a pajama top by the time he reached the squadron headquarters—and put it on. He stood in front of the small mirror on his locker and looked to ensure the captain's bars were positioned correctly and the pilot wings were level. He took his flight cap from the top shelf of the locker and, pushing the crush into the back, placed it on his head. The new wing commander, like Major Dynia, was a stickler for regulations and disliked the "fighter pilot crush," as the 'V' at the back of the hat was called. But there were a few who could get away with wearing their hats in this non-regulation and highly nonchalant style. Thibodeaux was one of those people. His Air Force Cross and his Purple Heart gave him the right to wear his hat any way he damn well pleased.

He wasn't proud of the Purple Heart; in fact, he had tried to decline it. Somehow he just couldn't feel right about claiming he had been wounded when all the doctors had done was pick some plexiglass out of his neck, shoulder, and forearm. "Hell," he thought, "only two of the places even required more than a stitch to close." He'd been hurt worse fighting crabapple duels as a kid. Still, one of the pieces *had* just missed his left carotid artery.

It had been Stretch who had absorbed the majority of the plexiglass and concussive force of the shell. After repair, his left leg looked like a patchwork quilt of skin pieces, with suture and stitch marks running every which way. He had hobbled around on crutches for the longest time, and then finally made his way back to the cockpit. When Stretch took his return-to-flying-status check rides, Thibodeaux had made sure the check rides were qualification flights for aircraft commander and not copilot. Stretch liked the upgrade so much he had volunteered to serve another tour. "Just in case," he said, "the war goes hot again."

The Marines rescued by Thibodeaux and Stretch on their last flight together had also all returned to active duty. Thibodeaux made it a habit to keep track of the people his crew had saved. Each of them, so far, had remained "saved."

"So, I've got a better record than most priests." He chuckled at his own joke.

Following what had been his morning routine for most of the past 357 days, he stopped at the little kiosk across the street from the flight line and ordered a fried egg sandwich and a carton of milk. He took these to his office in squadron headquarters, placed them on his desk, and then made his way down the hallway that, if possible, smelled even more of wood rot and mildew than it had last year.

He addressed the duty officer. "Take me off the board for deployment tomorrow. I'm DNIF for the foreseeable future." He pronounced the acronym D-nif. "In fact, since I'm a single digit midget—so close to departure—just take me off the board."

"Who's being taken off the board?" This from the soon-to-be-much-overweight Major Dynia who was coming out of his office on the back side of the duty desk area, his uniform shirt pulling across the buttons.

"Me." Thibodeaux turned away from the large scheduling board to face the short, round man whose very short legs made his stride appear to be that of a hurrying cartoon character.

The major, jealous of his position, as always was quick to confront. "How do you know you're DNIF? Have you seen the flight surgeon? You know only I have the authority to remove people from duty status. As the assistant operations officer, you're required to clear any changes to duty status with me before making them official, especially since I'm the acting squadron commander."

It was true. Lt. Colonel Abruzzi had flown back to the States to have a cyst removed from his right elbow. He had been gone for almost three weeks and would likely not return before Thibodeaux left for his new assignment. For Thibodeaux, those three weeks as the de facto number two in the squadron had been absolute hell. No wonder he had come down with a sinus infection. The major was a martinet, and so detail-oriented that he often missed the greater purpose of a mission by allowing himself to be distracted by unimportant items that others would have let slide. Still, it was only a week more. Why poke the guy with a stick?

Thibodeaux pulled the flight surgeon's form from the small portfolio he carried and handed it to the major, formalizing his DNIF status. At that moment he decided not to attempt to be removed from the DNIF list prior to departing base on his permanent change of station orders. No way did he want back on the flying duty roster. He would bite his tongue for this Johnny-come-lately this time, just as he had swallowed his bile so many times before during the major's two months in country, but his temper was growing short. He realized the major had a major inferiority complex, but still he was annoyed. It was the mental image of "the major" having a "major complex" that allowed him to pass this latest confrontation off as he had the others. He smiled.

After reading the form, the major pronounced, "Take Captain Thibodeaux off the duty roster."

At that moment the Blue Meanie walked into the duty area. "What do you mean, take Thibodeaux off the duty roster? I have his crew on my list for an unscheduled check ride for the deployment flight tomorrow."

Thibodeaux smiled. This was better than he could have hoped. He had managed to upset Major Dynia and the Blue Meanie at the same time.

Captain Mecham, known behind his back as "the Blue Meanie," looked hard at Thibodeaux who smiled back at him.

"You know you won't be current if I don't certify you before you leave?" Mecham spoke loudly so everyone down the hallway extending off the duty area could hear.

"Absolutely. But since I'm going to a school next, I don't need to be current. I'll be checking out on a number of different aircraft. So, thanks for the offer of a check ride, but I'll pass." Thibodeaux's smile, and the possible double meaning of his phrase, "I'll pass," seemed to put the Blue Meanie even more on edge, but when Thibodeaux pulled the handkerchief from his pocket and blew his nose, everyone laughed. Everyone, that is, except the major and Mecham.

Holding up the soiled kerchief, Thibodeaux announced, "Rest, ampicillin, and lots of liquids. That's what the doctor ordered. So..." he said, folding the kerchief and putting it in his portfolio instead of his pocket, "who wants to drive this poor, sick pilot back to his hooch?"

"Before you go, Captain, I want to see you in my office." The major did not ask, nor did he suggest. He ordered.

Passing through the portal, the major again ordered, "Close the door."

Thibodeaux wondered how the major hadn't learned, in his two months at base, that closing the door did nothing to stop the people on the other side from hearing the conversation. Plywood walls, especially plywood walls that had been up for years and that had rotted in the middle, did little for sound abatement.

The major turned to face Thibodeaux. Hands on his spreading hips, he asked, "About these night flights you take every other week or so. What do you do?"

"Do? Sir? We train, and we recalibrate the night recovery system equipment. It's fairly sensitive to all sorts of things like vibration, changes in temperature and humidity…so it takes a lot of effort to keep it up to ARRS Manual 60-1 specifications. Since Captain Spencer"—he almost said Stretch—"and now Lieutenant Boyer and I are the only qualified NRS functional check flight pilots, we have to keep the four aircraft within operating specs. Because the aircraft are also flown on day missions by non-NRS qualified crews, we spend a lot of time undoing and redoing calibrations that are caused by those non-NRS crews. And now, sir, I'm feeling a little rocky, so if you don't mind, I'm going back to my hooch and rack out."

"Oh, but I do mind, Captain. And, by the way, I suggest you not lie to me about what you do. I have a friend in the C-130 squadron at Ubon who told me he flew a night mission as an observer, and when they refueled your aircraft he noticed the side placards with the star and bars were missing. Now, why would your placards be missing?" The major looked like a prosecuting lawyer surprising a defendant with information that destroyed a well-crafted alibi. Major Dynia leaned forward, his face red, his legs wide apart, his hands on those spreading hips. The caricature came more into focus for Thibodeaux. He looked like a cartoon Mussolini.

Thibodeaux's earlier assumption that the night missions would no longer be his problem vaporized with the major's query. His suggestion to the CIA that they brief the major on the operation had been considered, but then turned down after the Agency ran the major's name through its files. Somewhere, somehow, Major Dynia had fallen into a state of bad grace with the CIA. "Not surprising," Thibodeaux thought to himself. Then he carefully considered his response. All he could come up with was, "I'm sure I can't answer that for you, sir. Perhaps your friend simply did not see the placards. After all, it was dark and probably moonless. Plus, the placards are black, and we are always forty feet from the C-130's windows during refueling." Thibodeaux's response was measured.

"There's nothing wrong with my friend's eyesight. It's perfectly good. You land somewhere and take the placards out of their holders. What else do you do?"

"I'm sure I can't answer that for you, sir." Thibodeaux did not like being pressed, and he tried to deflect the question. "Perhaps this is something you should discuss with the squadron commander."

"I *am* the squadron commander!" The major now had Thibodeaux behind the proverbial eight ball. Thibodeaux wished for the quick return of Lt. Colonel Abruzzi, but said, "Sir, I can only repeat that I cannot answer your question."

"Cannot or *will* not?" The major was angry, but then, he was always angry. It was his defense against the world.

"Definitely *cannot,* sir. All I can say is that my crew and I are not engaged in anything illegal. We fly night training and NRS calibration functional check flights. We perform a series of night recovery profile maneuvers to ensure the equipment is functioning as required by ARRS Manual 60-1. If we determine it isn't functioning to specifications, we reset and recheck until it performs within the specified limits. I might mention here, sir, such flights are required by ARRS Headquarters. There's even an order specifying the requirement for these flights in the squadron operating procedures notebook." Once again, Thibodeaux's response was measured, his voice slow, and, more importantly, low.

"Captain, I am giving you a direct order to tell me what you and your crew do on those flights. These are my aircraft and I want to know if you're smuggling contraband across foreign borders."

If the major had stopped with the direct order, Thibodeaux would have been in a more difficult position, but the continuation about owning the aircraft gave him an out. The major decidedly did not "own" the aircraft. The squadron commander had signed as the responsible party for the aircraft when he took command, but the planes were the property of the Aerospace Rescue and Recovery Service and the United States Air Force. As acting commander,

Major Dynia hadn't signed for anything, and acting commanders were not supposed to change any in-place procedures or regulations during their short stints as "commander in place of..."

Still, Thibodeaux was stuck, because if he pointed out that the major didn't have the authority to countermand an order given by higher headquarters, the major would just push further, and Thibodeaux would have, in a small way, identified that a higher authority had given him orders the major did not know about. He doubted the major would believe such orders existed, and this would only lead to more questions. So Thibodeaux, knowing full well how it would be received, said, "Major, in response to your direct order I will answer in as direct a manner as I know how. Sir, my crew and I are flying night missions to train on and calibrate the Night Recovery System on specific night recovery aircraft that are listed on the table of organizational assets of the ARRS. We are flying these missions in direct response to an Air Rescue and Recovery Service order issued by the deputy chief of staff for operations, ARRS Headquarters. I assure you we are doing nothing more with the aircraft than we have been ordered by ARRS Headquarters."

"I don't believe you. Why do you take the placards out?"

"Major, I have answered your question and informed you that all procedures are in accordance with the directives of ARRS Headquarters. I can do no more."

"Oh? Yes, you can, and you *will*. I'm placing you under house arrest for disobeying a direct order. I intend to go to the

Inspector General and ask for an investigation, and I will prefer charges as soon as the squadron commander returns."

Major Dynia did not seem to remember that Thibodeaux was scheduled to depart the base several days before the squadron commander was due to return. Countermanding departure orders that had already been issued by the military personnel center would require more than a little effort on the major's part.

"Captain, go to your quarters and consider yourself under house arrest!" The last sentence ascended in a crescendo that could be heard halfway down the flight line.

Thibodeaux rose on the balls of his feet, clicking his heels as he straightened himself. He almost gave a Nazi salute and said "*Yawhol, Herr Mayor,*" but again swallowed the insult. If he could swallow fear, insults were no problem. Still, this one tasted particularly nasty.

The duty area—normally a noisy place with radios crackling, teletypes clicking, and voices speaking over those ambient sounds—was suddenly as quiet as the fourteenth-century portrait room at the Metropolitan Museum. The only sound heard through the silence was a snicker of approbation from Captain Mecham.

As Thibodeaux stepped out of the major's office, he addressed the assembly, "So, who's going to take this sick pilot to his quarters?"

From the edge of what had now become a significant group, the diminutive Jésus stepped out. "Gotcha here, Captain, if you don't mind riding in the maintenance truck."

"Not at all, Sergeant. Not at all." And the two strode off down the hall, Jésus walking faster in a futile effort to keep up with the head-taller Thibodeaux—who stopped only long enough to pick up his sandwich and milk, and to remark, "Man does not live by bread alone. Sometimes he likes an egg in between."

As they climbed into the pickup, Jésus was beside himself. "Shit! Jean-Louis, what you gonna do?"

Jean-Louis, feeling increasingly bad from the sinus infection, answered calmly. "After you drop me off, I want you to find Stretch and bring him to my hooch," he said, referring to the shipping container he shared as a room with another captain.

"We'll see how the major likes dealing with our friends from you-know-where. By the way, is that flight to Udorn still on the board?"

"Flight to Udorn? Oh, you mean the flight to drop off the parts for the HH-43s over there. Yeah, it's still on for a 1400 departure."

"Ok, when you go back, add Stretch's name to the manifest. He's not on the schedule to do anything else, so nobody will mind him deadheading over and back. When you bring him to my quarters, stand by to take him back up to the flight line."

"Roger," was Jésus' only reply.

Twenty minutes later, Stretch knocked on Jean-Louis' door. When Jean-Louis opened it, his face was red from the hot washcloths he had been applying to his sinuses. The cloths were lying in a basin of water he had fetched from the bathhouse. He assumed house arrest allowed him use of the bathhouse—even if it was around the corner from his room.

After an appropriate amount of bemoaning the morning's events, Stretch, like Jésus, asked what there was to do.

"Well, Peter," Jean-Louis used Stretch's given name, "we're going to fight a direct order with a direct order. Or at least I think we are. Here's a note I wrote to the CIA station chief in Udorn. You need to hand it to him personally. It explains I'm under house arrest and such, and asks them to communicate directly with whomever at Rescue Headquarters they're using as a contact. I expect there are only two, the commanding general and the deputy chief of staff for operations. With any luck, I'll be done with this conundrum by noon our time tomorrow, and it will become your problem. Remember to press them for immediate action, otherwise that Falstaff of a buffoon may trip over more information about the program."

Stretch went off to play his part, indignant with the major and all others who threatened his good friend and mentor.

Thibodeaux had done what he could. He had violated neither the compartment of the operation nor his standing orders. He knew how seriously the CIA took their top secret operations. He wondered what damage might result from Major Dynia's explosion and whether there might be collateral damage as well. In the back of his mind he hoped it would be good for the squadron and Rescue, for he had developed a real fondness for many Rescue personnel, especially the line maintenance crews, flight engineers, and pararescue jumpers.

He found many of them truly personable and full of good humor. As for the pilots, there were four or five with whom he clicked, but for the most part he found them too wrapped up in themselves and their careers. For pilots, everything was about comparison and competition. They all wanted Air Force careers and they all wanted to be generals. Jean-Louis had not decided what he wanted to be, but he was pretty sure it wasn't an Air Force general. Still, he had four more years until his initial commitment expired—so he had some time to think about it.

As he lay in the sun of the Thai midday, he thought about life. He wasn't all that worried about the current situation since he knew he would win. He was a little concerned about the down-line consequences of the stories squadron members might tell. Many had heard his dressing-down by the major, and that story would certainly be embellished and retold. Still, worrying wasn't a good thing to do. He smiled slightly at the thought that he must be the only officer ever to be placed under arrest twice in one year—although he had never truly been arrested after the radio incident with the brigadier general. That possibility had been squashed quickly by the commanding general at Seventh Air Force when his aide suggested it would look pretty stupid to allow one of their generals to prefer charges in a situation where, if his order had been followed, an American airman would have been captured and likely killed by North Vietnamese forces. Instead, the Seventh Air Force had concurred in the recommendation that Captain Thibodeaux receive a Silver Star for his actions that day.

This, and other things, occupied Thibodeaux's mind as he baked his body and, more importantly, his sinuses, in the hot sun. For example, he was intrigued by the way his professional life had developed. He had joined the Air Force because he wanted to fly jets and be a test pilot. Well, he had flown jets for about three months, and then fate had stepped in and he had become a helicopter pilot in Rescue. Rescue could only be described as the best mission you could have if you absolutely had to go to war. And now—well, now—was the intriguing part. He had orders to attend both the Navy's rotary wing test pilots' school at Pawtuxet Naval Air Station in Maryland and the Army's test training program at Fort Rucker in Alabama. So he would be a test pilot after all; just not a test pilot who probed the edge of space in an X-15. His work would be attempting to overcome the deadly retreating blade stall phenomenon that plagued helicopters and limited their speed to around two hundred miles an hour.

He slept for a while in the makeshift chaise lounge, rose, showered to remove the coconut tanning oil from his body, then settled in the shade to read his Arabic newspaper. It was more than a week old, having arrived only yesterday from his source in Beirut. He felt it important to keep using his language skills, otherwise the four years of college study would have been for naught. The Beirut newspaper helped him with both Arabic and French since it was a bilingual paper. He also had subscriptions to papers from Paris and Rome.

He thought some about languages and wondered whether perhaps Russian or German would have been better languages to have studied in college, or maybe Chinese. He didn't know why, but he felt more *sympatico* with the French, Italians, and Bedouins of North Africa and the Crescent. He had little interest in the Arabs of the Arabian Peninsula, but, since that was where the oil was, he also glanced occasionally at a Saudi newspaper. Truth be known, he had little—if any—good feeling about the Saudis, just like he didn't really trust the Russians or, for that matter, the Israelis. These were just thoughts that ran through the back of his mind when he thought of those peoples.

Jésus brought him a meal of fried rice and spring rolls from the officers' club. It was his favorite and included some sticky rice with mango for dessert. Jésus tried to tell him about the reactions in the squadron headquarters and on the flight line to his now widely known confrontation with the major, but Thibodeaux did not want to hear. He did find it heartening that Jésus had blurted out that the flight line was murmuring mutiny against the major. If Jean-Louis had thought there was any serious chance of such an event he would have sent Jésus back with explicit instructions to defuse the situation, but he knew, one—that Jésus had likely inflated his description of attitudes and comments, and two—that flight lines loved to complain about commanders regardless of who those commanders were.

Jean-Louis climbed into his bunk, content with his actions and sure that things would work themselves out the way they should. He murmured his prayers for family and friends, and, with the aid of the medicine the flight surgeon had given him, fell into a dreamless sleep.

The knocking was heavy and loud. He struggled from under the sheet and mosquito net, catching one foot or the other two or three times before he was able to stand upright and move to open the door.

As the door opened, light swept into the windowless container. It was well after his normal waking time, but since he was under house arrest he had figured he would sleep as long as his body felt it needed. Apparently his body and whoever was at the door had different ideas about how much sleep was required.

It was Captain Porter, the squadron administrative officer.

When he looked at Thibodeaux all he could say was, "Jesus Christ, Jean-Louis! The acting squadron commander wants you in his office—now!"

Jean-Louis wasn't surprised. The major had probably received his instructions from Rescue Headquarters. The CIA had done its job.

Porter, unable to drag Jean-Louis to the office still wearing his sleeping shorts, had to wait while Jean-Louis washed his face, drug his electric razor over his face two or three times, and put on a clean, pressed uniform. After Jean-Louis finally took his hat from the upper shelf of the locker, Porter almost sprinted for the duty pickup parked on the road.

Word had spread quickly through the squadron, and everyone who could do so had created a reason to be in the headquarters building. When Thibodeaux walked down the hall towards the operation officer's office at the back of the building, only a few acknowledged him. Some avoided making eye contact, as if he had contracted some type of contagious disease that could be passed through his gaze.

The door to the office was open. He knocked on the jamb. He entered on command and stood at attention in front of the desk. The major stood in the corner near the single window. In his hand, he was holding what appeared to be a teletype cable from which he had been reading, probably for the tenth or eleventh time. Maybe it was actually the hundredth or two hundredth time. The paper looked as if it had been crumpled and then straightened, perhaps more than once.

The major crossed to his desk and, from a notebook, took a sealed, legal-sized envelope that he thrust at Thibodeaux. "This is for *you*." The "you" dripped disdain.

The envelope was from the message center and was marked, "Eyes Only—Captain Jean-Louis Thibodeaux." He inserted his finger under the flap and tore the envelope left to right. He unfolded the enclosed message. It announced itself as being from the Commanding General, Air Rescue and was a terse order that "upon receipt of this message, Captain Jean-Louis Thibodeaux will assume temporary command of the squadron until appropriately relieved." It carried all the correct numbers—his service number, his social security number, and an order number—and was "by the command of."

"Happy?" The major's question couldn't have been more accusing.

"Happy, sir? I don't know what you mean."

"Oh, the whole base knows I've been recalled for consultations with Rescue Headquarters. I don't know what you've done, but I know you're responsible for this. I warn you, Captain, I have lots of friends in the Air Force. The same friends who got me this assignment when Rescue didn't want me, and I assure you, I'll be talking with them."

Thibodeaux thought to make response, but knew any response he made now would be wrong. He could not feel sympathy for the major, and this last admission only increased Jean-Louis' sense that the major's current assignment was above his capabilities. "So," Jean-Louis thought, "Rescue never wanted Major Dynia." Thibodeaux's opinion of the personnel office at Air Rescue Headquarters jumped several notches.

Hearing Dynia's inadvertent confession, Thibodeaux was thankful for the rotten plywood walls of the office. He knew the major would not be returning from the upcoming consultations. He would be relieved, and, if eligible, retired. If he wasn't eligible to retire, he would be assigned to some minor support function at a remote site. The Air Force did not like being embarrassed by its officers in front of the CIA. Even a relatively junior captain like Thibodeaux knew that. He assumed the crumpled message the major held informed him to take first available transport. That would be tomorrow's daily Klong flight, the flight Thibodeaux had hoped to take in four days. Now, of course, he would have to wait until he was "appropriately relieved."

Well, he was almost going home.

CHAPTER 10

HOMEWARD BOUND

THE EARLY MORNING SUNSHINE STREAMING through the rice
bird's grime-covered windows created the feeling of being inside a grain silo. Each bit of husk floating in the air was illuminated, almost spotlighted, by the sun's rays. There were
millions of pieces of rice husk in the air, and each time Jean-
Louis moved across one of the stuffed rice bags more husks
wafted upward into the aircraft's cargo compartment to float
about until caught by some of the moving air that, in streaming through various loose-fitting fuselage seams, created multiple swirls and patterns throughout the DC-3's interior. He had
read about grain silo explosions caused by such chaff igniting.
"Wouldn't it be a hoot," he thought, "to have lived through the
hell of small arms fire, anti-aircraft shrapnel, and surface-to-air
missiles only to die in the explosion of a flying rice silo?"

The engines rumbled, occasionally rocking the heavily
laden airplane as the props slipped out of synchronization.
The bags of rice were much harder than he had thought they
would be. They almost made him long for the web seats of the

Klong Bird—almost. This airplane was slow, and the trip to Bangkok would take longer than expected since the flight had been forced to skirt some leftover thunderstorms just north of Ubon. Still, it would get him to Bangkok several hours ahead of the afternoon Klong flight. This would allow him to catch Pan American Flight 2 to Karachi. From Karachi he would take a Turkish Airways flight to Istanbul, and finally a Middle East Airlines flight to Beirut. This was only the beginning of a long trip. He needed to get comfortable.

No *sawatdi* leis hung around his neck, and no revelers had assembled for the 0430 departure. Stretch, Jésus, and Sergeant Sargent had wanted to see him off, but he told them he did not like goodbyes, and that he preferred to have one last drink the evening before his departure. So they had gathered in Thibodeaux's room and toasted friends present and past. Jean-Louis gave each of them a Seiko sterling silver dress watch on which had been inscribed, *"Chuc May Man,"* then sent them on their way. He knew they would respect his wishes.

So there had been no champagne or cheers as he headed out to the DC-3 that would take him to Bangkok. No one had even seen him go, for this aircraft had departed from the Thai Air Force cantonment at the very remote end of the long flight line. The squadron would open for business to find that he simply was no longer there and would not be departing via the Klong flight on that or any other day. He left in the dark, befitting his status as the senior night flier—only this time he flew south, not north.

Lt. Colonel Abruzzi had returned on the Klong Bird the day before and had "appropriately" relieved him of command.

So released, Thibodeaux had checked the base flight operations board for any aircraft that would get him to Bangkok in time to catch the same day's Pan Am flight. If he waited for the Klong, he would have had to switch all his travel reservations, and that could have trapped him for three days in Karachi and two days in Istanbul. By taking the Thai rice bird that morning, he could keep to his schedule—allowing him maximum time in Beirut, Rome, and Paris. He had booked a room at the Commodore Hotel in Beirut, the Hotel Eden in Rome, and the Hotel Westminster in Paris. While he intended to fly from Beirut to Rome, he planned to take the train from Rome to Paris, another train to the coast, and finally a ferry to England. In London, he planned to stay with a friend who was studying at the London School of Economics.

He had almost two months. No more generals, no more majors, no more blue meanies. He would remove the insignia from his uniform at the airport in Bangkok and leave the pants, shirt, and black oxfords in the trash. He had shipped all his flight gear and other necessaries in his allowed airfreight, so that morning he had only two pairs of chinos, two polo shirts, some underwear, socks, and a pair of brown suede chukka boots for the trip. He planned to purchase other clothes only as needed.

On this flight, though, he needed to make himself as comfortable as he could on the tightly packed two-hundred-pound gunnysacks of rice headed from the paddies of northeast Thailand to the markets of Bangkok. He scrambled over the tops of the piles until he found three bags not so well stacked.

There was a body-sized indentation between them. He slipped into this half cocoon, folded his hat across his eyes, and quickly fell into the sleep of an addict not yet free from the drug that had coursed through his veins for the past 378 days. He dreamed in an umber tint of unlit alleys, spies, narrow escapes, beautiful women, fast cars, and anonymous death.

Some say we cannot see the future, but that is not true. Some of us can see the future clearly. It is umber-colored, and passes before us as a movie in a dream.

Epilogue

THE DOCTORS FROM "BETWEEN HEAVEN and Hell" continued to treat those whose bodies and souls were ravaged in the service of their country.

Captain Komenda did not fly again. He did, however, become a five-term member of the U.S. House of Representatives. He died of a brain aneurysm that originated behind the stainless steel plate in his forehead. He was survived by his wife, Linda, and his son, Robert Fowler Komenda, who became an Air Force lieutenant colonel and F-15 pilot.

Pickerton was paroled after ten years, in no small part because Thibodeaux petitioned the parole board. He changed his name and became a licensed social worker in Washington D.C. where, among other things, he worked with veterans from the Gulf and Middle Eastern conflicts suffering from Post-Traumatic Stress Disorder. He knew the feeling of walls pressing in.

Captain Johnson never flew again. He was medically retired, earned a PhD in history, and became an assistant professor at a large Midwestern university.

The major from down the hall in "Between Heaven and Hell" was called before a court martial and dishonorably discharged for dereliction of duty and conduct unbecoming an officer and a gentleman. Two years later he committed suicide while drunk.

Airman Fowler died of bone cancer, a month shy of his twenty-second birthday. It was on a Wednesday. Yes, definitely Wednesday, because they had chicken soup and brussels sprouts—and there's no mistaking the smell of brussels sprouts. The Air Force presented his parents with his Air Force Cross, his Purple Heart, and the flag that covered his casket. While his funeral was small, many who could not attend grieved his death and celebrated his life.

The Marine H-46 crew and reconnaissance team from "Over the Top" all recovered from their injuries and returned to duty.

Tran Duc Dan, aka Danny Tran, retired from the CIA after a long career. He enrolled in cooking school in Paris where he learned to be a chef, and then he opened a small hotel in New Hampshire. Maybe you've eaten some of Danny's *foie gras* without realizing that it was made by a super-secret, super-successful spy.

The Vietnamese brother and sister were relocated, after a year, to the United States. With help from friends of the Agency, the sister found work in New York's high fashion sector while the brother traveled the world—first as an understudy to Danny Tran, and then in his own right as a spymaster. The two later moved to New Hampshire where they became part owners of a small hotel.

Sergeant Sargent retired from the Air Force as Chief Master Sergeant Sargent. He opened a dive shop in Key West.

The number two PJ on Thibodeaux's crew left the Air Force and became first a paramedic, then a physician's assistant, and finally a doctor. He worked as an emergency room physician in Montana.

Jésus recovered from his minor flesh wound and returned to flying well before Thibodeaux left the squadron. He was later assigned to the H-53 test squadron. He died in an accident during a test flight when the pilot overestimated his ability to fly the aircraft.

Lieutenant Colonel Schaffer and Lieutenant Colonel Abruzzi both made full colonel before retiring. They both went into commercial aviation, running small local aviation companies supporting regional carriers.

Major Dynia wasn't eligible to retire, so he was reassigned as an assistant administrative officer for a missile support unit at Minot Air Force Base, North Dakota. He retired as soon as he was eligible, and began selling insurance in Kansas City, Kansas.

Stretch, aka Lieutenant—then Captain—Peter Spencer, recovered from his wounds which had been numerous but not serious. He flew a second tour in Indochina as an aircraft commander and an NRS functional check pilot, and replaced the blue meanie as the chief of standardization and evaluation for the squadron. He later became a fighter pilot and a squadron commander, and then one of the youngest-ever wing commanders. When eventually faced with a decision between doing either the right thing or the politically correct thing, he asked himself, "What would the Captain do?" He did the right thing, and it cost him his shot at general. He retired as a colonel and became a senior vice president with a risk management company. You may have seen him on a major television news channel speaking of doing business in Russia and China.

Thibodeaux flew a tour as a test pilot evaluating new engine and rotor configurations, and, for a short time, he held the helicopter speed record. He was promoted to major and selected as a general's *aide-de-camp*. That was his last assignment before resigning from the Air Force. His resignation came as a surprise to his contemporaries who had assumed he was a lifer.

He didn't maintain contact with any of his former Air Force colleagues, and he never came to any Jolly Green reunions. At one reunion, his name came up and someone claimed to have seen him in a hotel in Cairo. But when they asked the concierge about the man they had seen, they were told it was an Italian businessman, a Señor Conti. Someone else claimed a similar experience during a trip to Katmandu. At the airport, they had seen someone they thought was Thibodeaux loading gear into a Pilatus Porter. But when they asked if anyone knew Thibodeaux, they learned that the pilot of the Porter was a Lebanese national flying supplies to a geological exploration team up near the Tibetan border.

Still, both former colleagues swore they thought they had seen Thibodeaux—because they had never seen anyone else with such emerald-green eyes.

But that is another story.

ABOUT THE AUTHOR

TONY JORDAN IS A HIGHLY decorated former senior officer of the Central Intelligence Agency's National Clandestine Service and an award-winning author.

Prior to joining the CIA, he was a rescue helicopter pilot in Southeast Asia and also served as an instructor, a test pilot, and a squadron commander in the US Air Force. From the jungles of Southeast Asia to the headquarters of the CIA, MI5, and MI6—with remote deserts, smoke-filled rooms, and dangerous back alleys in between—Jordan was involved in special military operations and covert intelligence work for more than forty years.

He now writes from the tower office of his cottage on Spy Hill Farm, in the foothills of the Crab Orchard Mountains of Tennessee, where he is ably supported and appropriately encouraged, when needed, by his wife, Anne, and his BFF, Tailwagger Jack.